"If it's an Abbott, it's mine."

Cordie had a horrible feeling that she understood what Killian meant, but she had to be sure. "You said you didn't want to reconcile."

"That's right," he told her.

She folded her arms so he wouldn't see her hands tremble. "You'll keep me until the birth, then take the baby away from me?"

"We'll work out a deal."

Without thinking twice, she struck him hard on the shoulder. "You don't deal over a baby." To herself she added, *This isn't part of the plan. You're supposed to invite me back into your life!*

"I'm not giving up my claim to the baby," Killian said unequivocally.

"It's mine!"

"It's ours. And trying to pretend I don't figure in his life isn't going to work."

She was suddenly aware that her plot had a serious pitfall. Killian was going to fight her for the baby. And he had an army of lawyers.

"You're hateful," she said in a heartfelt whisper.

He gave her a brief nod, as though it was of no consequence. "I gathered you felt that way when you slept with Brian."

Dear Reader,

The Hamptons on Long Island, New York, have always held a fascination for me. My only experience with the area is what I've seen at the movies or in decorating magazines. I love the notion of a sprawling, beachy house decorated in shabby chic and fronted by lawn and sea grass that meanders to the ocean. I can visualize Japanese lanterns, smell clam boils and barbecues, and hear music and laughter.

Of course, my writer's mind has to populate this place. I decided upon three brothers who've inherited the family wealth and business, but still bear guilt over a little sister who went missing twenty-five years earlier.

In my imagination, this sunny upscale place became Losthampton, and I created Killian, Sawyer and Campbell Abbott to live there with various members of their household and staff. Over the course of this series they will attract three strong, wise women who help them heal, and make their lives more interesting—and surprising—along the way.

Thank you for wanting to know them.

Best wishes!

Muriel

P.O. Box 1168
Astoria, Oregon 97103

Books by Muriel Jensen

HARLEQUIN AMERICAN ROMANCE

866—FATHER FOUND
882—DADDY TO BE DETERMINED
953—JACKPOT BABY*
965—THAT SUMMER IN MAINE

*Millionaire, Montana

HIS BABY
Muriel Jensen

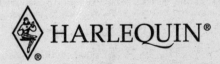

HARLEQUIN®

TORONTO • NEW YORK • LONDON
AMSTERDAM • PARIS • SYDNEY • HAMBURG
STOCKHOLM • ATHENS • TOKYO • MILAN • MADRID
PRAGUE • WARSAW • BUDAPEST • AUCKLAND

ISBN 0-373-75024-2

HIS BABY

THE ABBOTTS—A GENEALOGY

THOMAS and ABIGAIL ABBOTT (arrived on the *Mayflower*; raised sheep outside of Plymouth)

WILLIAM and DEBORAH ABBOTT (built a woolenmill in the early nineteenth century)

JACOB and BEATRICE ABBOTT (ran the mill and fell behind the competition when they failed to modernize)

JAMES and ELIZA ABBOTT (Jacob's eldest son and grandfather of Killian, Sawyer and Campbell; married a cotton heiress from Virginia)

NATHAN and SUSANNAH STEWART ABBOTT (parents of Killian and Sawyer; Nathan diversified to boost the business and married Susannah, the daughter of a Texas oilman who owned Bluebonnet Knoll)

NATHAN ABBOTT and CHLOE MARCEAU (parents of Campbell and Abigail; renamed Bluebonnet Knoll and made it Shepherd's Knoll)

KILLIAN ABBOTT is married to CORDELIA MAGNOLIA HYATT

His brothers are SAWYER and CAMPBELL

His sister, ABIGAIL, is still missing

Chapter One

Killian Abbott strode to the small bar behind his desk while Jack Eagan went on with his report. Jack was new, but proving to be the most competent human resources director Abbott Mills, Inc., had ever employed, so Killian listened with only one ear while he poured coffee and wondered what to do about the small chain of Florida clothing stores—Florida Shops—his stepmother wanted him to buy.

The investment wasn't a big one, just a couple of million dollars, but the acquisition would make Chloe happy because the owner was a friend of hers. Still, the purchase was a distraction he'd prefer not to deal with right now with a divorce in the works and the November Corporation always looking for a break in the wall to attempt a takeover of Abbott Mills.

"Productivity is up eleven percent in the mills, and sales are up more than twenty percent in the stores. We think the new gyms are responsible for some of that. Morale's up, injuries and accidents are down, and—" Jack, who'd stood when Killian had, stopped talking as Killian handed him a mug of coffee. "Mr. Abbott," he said with an air of distress. He was older and conscientious and had come to Abbott Mills with a long history of managing household staffs in England. "I wish you wouldn't wait on me, sir. It makes me nervous."

Killian pointed him back into his chair and sat on the edge of his desk with his own cup. "It makes *me* nervous when you stand every time I do. I'm not titled gentry, Jack, just your employer. And you don't have to call me 'sir.'"

"Yes, sir." At Killian's frown, Jack closed his eyes and groaned. "Even after two years at Southern Massachusetts University, studying business and psychology, I'm having trouble getting the drift of American ways."

"Just relax."

"Yes, sir."

Letting that issue drop for now, Killian indicated the file from which Jack read. "Go on. Productivity and morale are up. Good." Adding an exercise room to every Abbott Mills store and all other factories the corporation owned had been a good idea. "Injuries and absenteeism are down. I like that."

Jack held his cup uncomfortably and searched for his place in his notes with his index finger. "Mrs. Hamilton reports that the new cleaning firm we hired for the Dartmouth store is working out very well, as is the new buyer for women's wear, who came on board last month."

"All *good* news," Killian observed with a smile. "There now, that wasn't so bad."

Jack smiled with relief. Killian liked reports given in person rather than dry written reports read at board meetings, and this was Jack's first. Tall and thickly built, the man had the posture of a marine at fifty-six. When Killian had interviewed him, wanting the right man for the job, he'd asked him why he'd left England after almost a lifetime.

Jack had replied that he'd been widowed, and his only son had died in his teens in a riding accident. "I felt old and aimless," he'd admitted candidly, "and thought I needed new surroundings.

"I'm here to stay," he'd said. "You'll notice on my references that I was with the duke of Burrage for twelve years, until he lost the house to taxes. Then I spent twenty-two years in the service of Lord Dunnsford. I like to put down roots."

Killian had hired him. He, too, favored roots.

That had been almost three months ago, and he now considered it the smartest move he'd ever made as CEO of Abbott Mills.

Except for Jack's tendency to treat him like royalty.

The coffee was good—a Zimbabwe blend his secretary, Barbara Garrett, had bought at a little coffee roaster's on the ground floor of the Abbott Building. The personnel report was good—one more thing he wouldn't have to worry about in the next few months. And the sun warming his back through his midtown Manhattan window was good, reminding him how nice getting home this weekend, maybe logging some time on the beach, would be.

Jack sighed, obviously pleased. "I'm glad that's over, sir. Mr. Abbott."

"But you have to stop thinking of coming to this office as an appearance before the throne. We're a pretty democratic company.

"Here we all work together in the service of our customers, so to speak. You'll relax after you've spent time with everyone at our annual meeting."

Jack looked doubtful. "I was told it's at your home on Long Island this year. Is that true?"

"Yes. We usually get together at a big hotel to meet new members of the staff, look over Abbott Mills's new products and plan strategy for next year. Last year was great for Abbott Mills and I want everyone to know how much I appreciate the hard work. You'll give your report to the corporate staff and I think you'll have a good time."

"I will?" Jack's voice went up an octave.

"You will. You did this very well. You'll be fine. Everyone will stay for the weekend, enjoy the grounds and the beach. It's a painless way to get things done."

"Yes. Mr. Abbott."

Killian took the copy of Jack's report and perused it. "Anything else I should know about?"

"I don't think so, sir. The written report has a little more detail, but it all relates to the highlights I've already given you. The personnel picture is very good."

Killian nodded, flipping through the pages. He stopped when he came to the profile of the new employee in women's wear. She'd been a lucky find, so Jack had told him when he'd hired her as a buyer. She had an MBA and considerable experience in the fashion business. Jack had been enthusiastic about her people skills and her knowledge of— Oh, God!

Killian's hands froze on the report when his eyes ran over her previous experience. Buyer for Bloomford's department stores. Three years as marketing manager for Hyatt Furniture in Newport News, Virginia.

Hyatt Furniture!

Three years modeling for…André McGinty!

Dread rising in him, he reread the vital identifying information.

Name: Cordelia Hyatt.

Killian surged to his feet and said a few words Jack had probably not heard among the English gentry, judging by his sudden blanching. Killian slapped the report on his desk and turned to confront Jack, unable to believe the man had done this to him. He was not surprised to find that Jack, too, had gotten to his feet.

"What, sir?" Jack asked in a calm voice. "What is it? Whatever it is, I can fix it."

"You damn well better, Jack," Killian replied, temper barely held in check. "You just hired my wife!"

Jack stared at him for a confused moment. "You mean…the one you're…divorcing?"

"Yes, the one I'm divorcing!" Killian shouted. Then, remembering that he never shouted, he drew a breath and counted ten beats of his heart. That didn't take long; it was thumping. "How many wives do I have?" he asked reasonably. "Cordelia Hyatt is my wife."

"Forgive me, sir, but I didn't know that." Jack spoke quietly, though he appeared distressed. "When I was first hired, I'd heard rumors of your divorce after only three months, but I didn't know...I mean...I'd heard your wife was in Scotland. Brokenhearted, everyone said."

Brokenhearted. Killian glared at him. She had not been brokenhearted. She was just used to having things her way and she'd wanted him very badly. Losing him had simply been a disappointment. One she should have anticipated when she slept with Brian Girard, marketing manager of the November Corporation and son of Corbin Girard, its CEO.

The Girards and the Abbotts had been in serious competition for the upscale ready-to-wear market for years, and Killian's father and Corbin Girard had hated each other. Killian and Brian had always felt obliged to suspect each other because of that situation. That the press and society put them in opposite corners of the business ring contributed to their contentiousness.

The Girards had been threatening a takeover of Abbott Mills for several years now, and though Killian felt confident that the corporation was too secure for that to happen, the weight of responsibility for a business that had been in his family for over two hundred years made him worry anyway.

Jack squared his shoulders under Killian's stare. "That's what they said," he insisted. "How was I to suspect she'd be back wanting *employment?* And you must admit that this trend among American women to retain their maiden name contributes to this kind of confusion."

Killian had to grant him that. He went to the bar behind his desk, ignored the coffeepot and poured himself a shot of bourbon. "She did take my name," he said, gulping it down. It burned a trail down to his stomach but failed to provide the warming comfort he waited for. He had to acknowledge that it probably wasn't coming. And he had a meeting with his advertising rep in half an hour; he couldn't have a second drink. "I'm sure she took advantage of the fact that you were new to the company and wouldn't recognize her if she used her maiden name."

Jack asked quietly, "What do you want me to do, sir?"

There was only one answer to that question. "I want you to terminate her."

Jack stared at him a moment, then cleared his throat. "I'm sorry, Mr. Abbott, but you sounded a little like Tony Soprano there. Please define *terminate.*"

Killian looked into the man's eyes, wondering if he really doubted what he meant or if he was trying to inject a little humor into a tense situation. "Don't kill her, Jack," he replied gravely. "Just fire her."

"On what grounds, sir? I understand she's already struck a rapport with her staff and everyone they work with. She's booked at all the shows for the fall season. Trilby says there's a renewed dedication among the—"

Killian stopped him with a shake of his head. Trilby Brown was Jack's assistant and had been with Abbott Mills for seven of her twenty-seven years. She and Cordie had mutual friends and had known each other before Killian had met Cordie. "Trilby knows she was my wife," he accused. "And she didn't tell you?"

Jack shook his head and firmed his jaw. "She didn't, sir. In her defense I can only guess she thought you knew and approved of the hire."

Killian gave him a pitying look. "Tell me you don't really believe that."

Jack sighed. "I'm not sure, sir. There seems to be a cunning charm among American women that's outside my sheltered experience."

"Yeah." Killian put an arm around Jack's shoulders and led him toward the door. "Mine, too. On second thought, it isn't fair to ask you to handle this. I'll take care of it myself."

"But, it's my responsi—"

"No." Killian cut him off firmly. "Cordie is *my* responsibility. I'll handle her."

Now Jack gave *him* a pitying look.

Cordelia Magnolia Hyatt Abbott wielded the nozzle of a clothing steamer in the back room of the women's wear department of the Abbott chain's flagship store on Manhattan's Upper West Side, just a few blocks from the Abbott Building. She was surrounded by tops and pants in tangerine, limeade, sunshine and summer blue. The playful garments in cotton-candy colors had been shipped tightly packed and now required touching up before they could be put out on the sales floor.

This was her last chore in what had been a long day of unpacking and tagging new stock, and she couldn't wait to get home to her apartment and put her feet up. She should stop by the gym first and fit in a workout, but she wasn't up to it today. A wedge of sausage lasagna, raw veggies and dip from Rocco's Deli were much more appealing. Fattening, but appealing.

Perspiring from the steamer, she reached into the pocket of her protective smock for a tissue, then dabbed at her forehead and around her half glasses. With the one hand, she finished work on the last blue shirt.

Then she heard sounds of arrival beyond the curtain that separated the stockroom from the sales floor.

"Hi, Mr. Abbott!" That voice belonged to twenty-year-old Candy in the junior department, who thought their boss was a "major babe."

"Mr. Abbott! Hello!" Eleanor, in formal wear and now an assistant manager. She'd been with the company since Killian's father, Nathan Abbott, had run it, and she considered Killian "a dear."

"Hey, Mr. Abbott. How's it going?" Hunter, who'd been union shop steward at her previous job, had admitted to Cordie that she'd been disappointed to learn that Abbott Mills didn't have a union. Until she'd been around long enough to realize the company didn't need one. But she felt the need to watch out for any infractions of a labor-management nature. She thought Killian was "a model of modern administration."

To Cordie, he was all those things, as well as the beat of her heart, the breath in her lungs and the absolute love of her life. Unfortunately, he had issues that also made him a complete doofus where she was concerned. She'd let him drive her away three months ago, but she'd had time to rethink her reaction and plan strategy in the seven weeks she'd spent in her father's hunting lodge in Scotland.

So when Killian swept the curtain aside and invaded the stockroom, she faced him with a new resolve, born of her realization that even though he was completely wrong about her in every way possible, she loved him utterly and she was not going to let him ruin their lives as he was determined to do.

Actually, she was convinced it was his own life he was bent on destroying, but since hers was so woven into his, it would be ruined, too.

"Killy." She glanced at him with a friendly smile as she went on with her steaming. Secretly, she wished she weren't perspiring and wearing a messy smock. She'd wanted to be wearing a ball gown at a party when he saw her again, and looking gorgeous. But that had been a silly, self-indulgent thought. "What a nice surprise. What brings you to Abbott's West?"

She had to keep steaming, keep pretending that her heartbeat wasn't choking her and her hands weren't shaking. This plot to get him back had to work.

She'd hoped to find that the time spent without her had changed him. She was sad and a little hurt to see that it hadn't. He didn't appear tired or depressed, and there was no evidence of regret in the Paul Newman–blue of his eyes. Annoyance was clearly visible there, not regret.

His wavy light brown hair was brushed away from a high forehead in the same old way, strands of blond springing up despite the designer gel she'd bought him to try to keep his hair in order.

His features were also the same: a slash of eyebrows darker than his hair over those dramatic eyes; a strong, straight nose; square teeth in a mouth that at the moment was thin-lipped and tight, but that she knew could be warm and clever; a nicely shaped chin in a square jaw that matched the line of his broad, square shoulders.

He was very tall and very fit, and if she stepped up to him her cheek would rest against his chin.

But he'd hate that right now, and she'd had all the rejection she could stand for a while. That she'd applied for and charmed her way into this job meant she was willing to open herself up to rejection again—but not this minute.

"What do you think you're doing?" Killian demanded as he took several steps into the room. He wore one of the dozen Armani suits that filled his wardrobe, this one gray and quietly elegant.

She pretended surprise at the question and held up the steamer nozzle. "Working," she replied. "You require that of employees, as I recall."

He yanked the nozzle out of her hand and leaned down to turn off the machine before draping the hose over it. When he straightened, the last puff of steam lingered between them like mist in the last scene of a love story. But she guessed their story wasn't going to have a happy ending. At least not yet.

"I don't want you working for me," he said, folding his arms as he frowned down at her. "I can't believe you had the nerve to do this."

She, too, folded her arms, and regarded him with the same disdain he focused on her. "Well, you should have thought of that before you hired me."

"I didn't! A new employee who didn't know we'd been involved hired you."

She arched an eyebrow, proud of her cool demeanor. "Involved? We were married, Killian. That goes a step further than involvement."

He leaned his weight on one hip and mimicked her raised eyebrow. "Really. But not far enough to prevent you from sleeping with another man while you were supposed to be on a business trip. And not just any man, but a lifelong business rival."

She struggled for an even tone. This was the point where she could lose it. "I didn't sleep with him."

"You were in bed and he was leaning over you. You have a history."

"I told you..."

"That he'd let himself in. I remember. But you were in *his* room."

"I explained that, as well."

"Yes. Your room didn't lock and his did. You'd returned from a late dinner with others who'd come to Paris for the show, and you couldn't make the desk clerk understand the problem. So Brian switched rooms with you. That's lame enough to sound like damning evidence to me."

She drew a breath, prepared to advance the plan to save her marriage. Getting down and dirty. "That's because you want to believe the worst of me," she said, inclining her upper body toward his to make her point. "You were happy with me, Killian, and on some level I don't understand and you probably don't, either, happy doesn't work for you. You've chosen against it. You work night and day and offer up on the altar of your sister's disappearance whatever part of you might once have been fun."

He took a step toward her, his eyes darkening. "Don't speculate on what you don't understand," he threatened.

"Then *tell* me about it so I *do* understand!" she pleaded. "Explain to me what the kidnap of little

Abigail did to you. Let me close enough to help you!''

"I don't need you to do that," he said with alarming sincerity. "You're always trying to root around inside me and clean things up with your terminal good cheer. Well, you were like a...an aberration for me! I'm attracted to serious, stable women, not impulsive *ingenues* who laugh and party all the time as though life were just one big high.''

Hearing herself described as an aberration hurt, but she stood her ground and swallowed the pain. "You fell in love with me," she said unequivocally.

He denied that with a shake of his head. "At a difficult period in my life, I fell in love with the idea of escaping through you.''

She scoffed at that notion inelegantly by blowing air between her lips. "Escaping it, my aunt Fanny! You thrive on the crunch, Abbott! You love facing down the enemy and making him flinch. The November Corporation is never going to launch a successful takeover and you know it. Abbott Mills is too strong. Brian probably set up that whole hotel-room scenario to rattle you, and you fell for it because you *wanted* a reason to send me away. I was helping you forget business once in a while and that terrified you because it meant you had to be a real human being instead of a hard drive, a digital modem and a collection of sophisticated circuitry.''

Apparently unimpressed with her assessment of his personal makeup, he put a hand to his chest and asked calmly, "Well, if you're so offended by this machine, why did you apply for and accept a job here?''

''Because while I am offended by what you've turned yourself into,'' she replied candidly, ''I know the man you really are inside. And I want that man back.''

He stared at her for a moment in silent disbelief. Then his gaze hardened. ''I'm divorcing you,'' he said finally.

''I have to sign the papers,'' she reminded him.

He accepted that with a nod. ''If you refuse, that won't hold it up forever. Eventually, the divorce will be allowed, and that'll be that.''

''Yes,'' she admitted. ''But until that happens, I can live in hope that you'll wake up one morning and remember what life was like when you let yourself be happy. What it was like when we were together.''

Clearly surprised and angered by her stand, he opened his mouth to offer an argument, then seemed to change his mind. He turned and stalked away.

KILLIAN HEARD Cordie following him as he headed for the elevators. She ran around in front of him and walked backward as he kept going.

''Am I fired?'' she asked. ''You didn't say. Because I have scores of appointments with suppliers over the next few weeks and several critical shows scheduled for—''

Yes! he wanted to shout as she went on. But that little union troublemaker, Hunter, was pretending to sort through a rack of shorts while clearly tipping an ear in their direction. He didn't need November to hear rumblings among the employees of an unfair firing.

Jack's Soprano interpretation of *termination* would have been simpler than this, he acknowledged to himself grimly.

"No," he replied, pushing the Down button. "But I'll be going over your performance with a microscope. And I'll take advantage of the first excuse I can find to fire you." The elevator bell dinged and the doors parted. He stepped onto the car and turned to her with an air of dismissal. "Now, if you'll excuse me, I'm going down."

She looked into his eyes with a gleam in hers as the doors began to close. "Yes," she said. "You are."

Chapter Two

In the back seat of a Lincoln limousine, Killian took one last look at Abbott's market quotes, checked the status of his personal portfolio as well as Chloe's investments, then closed his laptop and put it aside with disciplined determination. He had to clear his mind this weekend. He could usually work sixteen-hour days for months at a time, but he hadn't taken a full weekend off since before the Cordie-Brian debacle and he was due.

He could forget about business for forty-eight hours. Chloe was spending the weekend in the city, his brother Sawyer had left yesterday for New Hampshire on a chore for the Abbott Mills Foundation and Campbell had left a message saying he was going to Florida to check out a position at Flamingo Gables, the summer home of the Elliott Prathers.

Great. He really didn't need his estate manager to quit at this point in time, but he knew his younger brother had issues with Shepherd's Knoll and no amount of reasoning with Campbell seemed to change his mind. Even Chloe's pleadings had been to no avail. So all Killian could do was let him go and hope that distance made Campbell's heart grow fonder of his half brothers and the headache that was Shepherd's Knoll, their family home.

"Finished for the day, Mr. Abbott?" Daniel Chambers asked from the front seat. He was African American, in his early sixties and wearing a dark business suit. Killian's father had hired him decades ago.

Initially, Nathan Abbott had refused to hire him because he'd refused to wear a uniform. Nathan had driven himself to town the morning after the interview and had an accident on the Long Island Expressway while trying to talk to his secretary on the car phone. He'd hired Daniel that afternoon.

"Yes," Killian replied, stretching out his legs. "You're not going to ask for investment advice again, are you?"

Daniel laughed. "Linus Larrabee gave Fairchild advice in *Sabrina* and the chauffeur had millions by the end of the movie."

"True. But it was the senior Mr. Larrabee who gave him advice, and Fairchild had a beautiful daughter for Linus to fall in love with."

"You're a married man!"

"Not anymore."

"Come on, Mr. Abbott. You're going to love Miss Cordie till the day you die. Only trouble is, you don't know how to live with her."

"God wouldn't know how to live with her. I don't need that kind of trouble."

Daniel didn't reply. That meant he disagreed. Killian felt alarmed at how little stock the family and staff put in Cordie's adultery. "You're supposed to humor me, Daniel," Killian teased. "Tell me I'm right, that women are generally no damn good—except for your Kezia, of course—and that *nobody* needs the kind of trouble they bring."

"Man's character is honed by trouble, Mr. Abbott," Daniel philosophized with a bright smile in the rearview mirror. "Your mother running off made a hardworking man out of your father. Otherwise, the way he was goin', he'd have gambled away your inheritance."

"But she *proved* the women-are-no-damn-good theory."

"Yep. Every once in a while there's one. Still, she's responsible for you and Mr. Sawyer bein' here, and that's no small thing. You make money like nobody's ever seen and Mr. Sawyer makes sure all the extra gets spread around, doing good work."

That might have been an oversimplification of the situation, but Killian liked the sound of it.

"Thank you, Daniel. By the way, you can have the weekend off. I'm not going back to town until Monday morning." Daniel lived with Kezia in what had once been the guest house.

"You sure about that, Mr. Abbott?"

"I'm sure."

Killian loved Shepherd's Knoll. He didn't spend

nearly enough time here now that Abbott Mills had holdings overseas, but he got the same feeling of security and history he used to get as a child when his father turned onto the long, poplar-lined driveway that led to the house.

On Sunday-afternoon drives around Long Island, Nathan Abbott used to tell Killian and Sawyer about Thomas and Abigail Abbott, who'd come over on the *Mayflower* and raised sheep outside of Plymouth. Over the generations, the frugal, clever Abbotts had prospered, and William Abbott had started a woolenmill early in the nineteenth century.

Jacob Abbott, Killian and Sawyer's great-grandfather, had continued to run the mill, but he'd fallen behind the competition when he'd failed to install new and more sophisticated machinery, considering it frivolous. His losses were considerable by the time he'd realized the error of his ways, but by then he didn't have the capital to purchase new equipment.

So James Abbott, Jacob's eldest son, had been encouraged to marry a cotton heiress from Virginia. New equipment and the new bride's knowledge of business had improved the Abbott fortunes considerably.

With the advent of synthetics in the middle of the twentieth century, Nathan, now in control of the company, had diversified. He'd married Susannah Stewart, the daughter of a Texas oil baron, and they'd moved to her family's summer home in Losthampton, New York, situated in the small cleft of an inlet on the south coast of Long Island between East Hampton and Southhampton.

When Nathan and Susannah Abbott had moved into her family's palatial home, it had been known as Bluebonnet Knoll because of the Stewarts' Texas connection. But when Susannah had run off with the chauffeur, giving Nathan the house to assuage her guilt over leaving her children, Nathan had changed the name, wanting it to reflect his family's business rather than hers.

Killian remembered his mother. Instead of warm, fuzzy recollections of a loving woman, he had strong, clear memories of a light-haired goddess always in gowns and sparkling jewelry, waving to him from across the room. She'd seldom come into the nursery, simply blown kisses from the doorway.

He'd harbored the hope that someday when he was big enough and smart enough, she'd come and talk to him, possibly even hold him. But that had never happened.

One day his father had called Sawyer and him into his study and told them their mother was gone and a new woman was coming into their lives. She was French, he'd said, and a designer for one of the clothing companies Abbott's owned.

Killian remembered clearly the shock and distress he'd felt at having to accept that the goddess would never get to know him, never hold him, that she was lost to him forever. He'd been five.

Someone had to pay, so he'd made the new woman, named Chloe, the culprit. He'd told her straight off that he didn't want anything to do with her, didn't want her in his house and didn't want her touching his brother.

Sawyer, though, even at three a man with a mind of his own, adored her instantly. Killian had resisted heroically, but had finally lost the battle to hate her when she'd walked into the nursery with his father about a week after her arrival and asked, "Is there a reason the children must be confined to this floor while we are home?"

His father had thought a moment. "Susannah liked it this way. She said it kept them out of her hair when her friends came around."

Chloe had shrugged. "Well, as I have no friends yet and…" She'd patted a very short haircut. "As I have no hair for them to get into, I don't see why they can't have the run of the house. Except for your office, of course, when you are working at home. The staff tell me they are very good children and usually behave themselves well." She'd put a hand to Killian's face and one to Sawyer's. It had been warm and smooth and had smelled of lilacs. "And you will continue to behave for me, *n'est-ce pas?*"

A whole new world had opened up. Although Susannah had never come back and Killian, ever her champion, had sat by his window every night before going to bed and watched for her, during the day he'd loved being with Chloe as much as Sawyer had. She took them everywhere—shopping, to church, to visit the friends she eventually made, to the beach. He'd maintained a locked-up corner of his heart for

Susannah, but he'd let Chloe in and allowed himself be happy again.

Campbell was born the following year and Abby, almost four years after that.

Killian smiled at memories of his big-eyed, plump-cheeked baby sister, then straightened in his seat and put all thoughts of her out of his mind. He wanted to relax this weekend, to refill the well of his usually nimble mind and steady focus.

Thoughts of Abby, and, of course, her disappearance, wouldn't allow that.

Daniel pulled around to the front of the house. Its cozy grandeur was somehow welcoming. To this day, Killian wasn't sure what to call the architectural style. His father had referred to it as Seaside Victorian. Unlike the many slope-roofed and angular federal-style homes in the region, this one had large, long windows all around, a tower on one side and a circular porch on the bottom of the tower, one on the second level where the tower connected to the main part of the house, and on the back of the top floor with its view of the ocean. The frame exterior was painted a cheerful butter yellow.

Winfield opened the front door before Killian could open it himself. Campbell had hired the former boxer a year ago as a sort of butler-bouncer. Campbell resented Killian's use of that term, insisting that Killian never took his vulnerability to theft or kidnap seriously.

Actually, Killian did. He'd thought about it every night since Abby had been taken almost twenty-seven years ago. But he didn't want someone around to remind him that that kind of thing could happen. And he was a much less likely target than a fourteen-month-old child.

"What about Mom?" Campbell had asked when Killian had denied he himself could be a target. "Sure, you're six foot three and trained in self-defense, but she isn't. And you're gone so much of the time."

Killian had conceded. For their stepmother to have protection in the guise of a butler was a good idea, and he knew Campbell remembered Abby's kidnapping, though he'd only been five and a half at the time. He was working out his own demons brought to life by the event.

So Killian cooperatively handed Winfield his briefcase and let him take his jacket.

"How are you, Mr. Abbott?" Winfield asked in a voice more suited to a boxing ring than a stately home. Though he was two inches shorter than Killian, he was probably twice as broad and all of it muscle. He had thin blond hair, pale blue eyes and a boxer's nose.

He'd caused a few second looks when he'd first opened the door to guests a year ago, but his courtesy and kindness had since won everyone over.

"I'm good," Killian replied. "How are you, Winfield?"

"Fine, sir. Though I'm worried about your mother."

"Why is that?"

"She's going to Paris, Mr. Abbott."

Killian, in the act of looking through the mail on the hall table, blinked at him. "Paris? I thought she was going to the city for the weekend."

"I was, I was!" High heels clicked down the marble floor as Chloe hurried toward them at a run slowed down by the beginnings of arthritis and her Prada shoes. She was small and graying, with a face filled with warmth. In a silk suit, with a hand-painted scarf trailing behind her, she was the picture of a society matron. "To stay with the Mitchells in their city condo and go to the theater. But their daughter's with the Ballet de Paris, and she sent them tickets for her *début*—" she gave the word its French pronunciation "—next week and they've invited me along. You know how I love the ballet. And I can visit Tante Bijou while I'm there!"

Tante Bijou was legendary in their lives. Chloe's mother's sister had been in the Resistance during World War II, had written a much-acclaimed book about her experiences and had married five or six times—even Chloe had lost count. She was Chloe's only living relative in France, and Chloe leaped at every opportunity to visit her.

"I was hired to protect you, Mrs. Abbott," Winfield said politely. "How can I do that when you're there and I'm here?"

Chloe rolled her eyes. They'd apparently been having this argument for some time. "I won't have you coming with me and leaving the boys here defenseless." Even she had difficulty keeping a straight face when she said that. Killian had boxed in college, Sawyer was a third-degree black belt and Campbell had a chip on his shoulder the size of Alaska and everyone seemed to know better than to mess with him.

Winfield faced her resolutely. "Mr. Campbell would insist…"

Killian patted Winfield's shoulder. "It's okay. Steve Mitchell was a marine," he said.

"Sir, he's in his sixties!"

Chloe slugged his arm. "So am I! And I'm hardly at death's door."

"I didn't mean…"

"I've golfed with him," Killian said. "He has quite a swing and considerable endurance. He'll take care of the ladies."

"I'll be *fine*," Chloe insisted.

Winfield opened his mouth to protest further, but Killian silenced him with an unobtrusive shake of the head.

Winfield appeared puzzled, but closed his mouth.

The doorbell rang and Winfield opened it to Steve Mitchell, who greeted Killian, then took Chloe's bag. She followed him out to a shiny black Cadillac, chattering incessantly.

"The minute they're out of sight," Killian whispered to Winfield, "we'll call your company and get someone to trail her and the Mitchells while they're in Paris." To his mother, he asked, "Where you staying, Mom?"

"At the Hôtel Clarion St-James et Albany. The

duke of Noailles once entertained Marie Antoinette there, you know.''

He raised an eyebrow at Winfield, who nodded, the data obviously stored in his memory.

''Good strategy, Mr. Abbott,'' Winfield praised under his breath.

''Never fight a battle you can't win,'' Killian replied, even as he blew Chloe a kiss.

That was good advice to apply to Cordie, he suddenly realized. But there was no such thing as a nonconfrontational way of dealing with her. She was a forthright, in-your-face kind of woman. Even Sun Tzu, the brilliant strategist, would have had difficulty dealing with her.

CORDIE FINALLY PUT her feet up at about eight o'clock. She sat on the sofa in her elegant, quiet-as-a-tomb apartment, alone except for her cat, and tried hard to be interested in the steaming square of lasagna on the tray in her lap. She'd anticipated it all afternoon, but now that she had the food, it made her stomach churn.

She put the tray aside and leaned her head back against the ticking-striped sofa cushion and wondered grimly if this was what had happened between her and Killian: that he'd found her less than interesting once he had her, and put her aside.

She hoped simple ego wasn't at work, but she couldn't believe he'd just lost interest in her. The kind of earnest determination with which he'd pursued her couldn't simply evaporate. The fervent passion with which he'd made love to her couldn't just cease to be.

A waning of interest had happened even before the Brian thing had given him an excuse to talk divorce. She'd caught glimpses of regret in his eyes, felt it in his touch when he pulled her to him on impulse and wrapped his arms around her, only to change his mind and push her away.

What had happened?

She'd racked her brain over the question all the time she'd spent in Scotland, but she hadn't come up with an answer. And the problem couldn't be solved without one. It would take time spent with him. Either the attraction that had drawn them together so explosively the first time would take hold again and last, or he'd react as he had the first time they'd met. In that case, she'd be on guard and able either to ward off his displeasure or figure out what brought it on and do something about it. Or not. But at least she'd understand.

Loving a man who didn't want anything to do with her was tough. Before she'd met Killian at his stepmother's fashion show for charity, she'd have considered herself the last woman on the planet who'd pursue a man who didn't want her. But gut instinct told her that he did still love her and that his sudden withdrawal from her was a self-inflicted punishment for some imagined guilt over Abigail's disappearance.

Kezia had told her the story shortly after Cordie and Killian's Thanksgiving wedding. Kezia and

Daniel had been working for the Abbotts less than a year one late December night when they were planning for a New Year's Eve celebration in two days' time. Killian, eleven years old, had been at a sleepover at a friend's house, and Sawyer, nine, Campbell, five, and fourteen-month-old Abby were asleep in their beds. Kezia had been up late baking pies when she heard the screams.

She and Daniel had run upstairs to find Kate Bellows, the nanny, pacing the second-floor hallway, screaming. She wore a billowing silk robe, her gray hair hanging in one long braid. '''She's gone!' she kept saying over and over. 'She's gone! I got up to go to the bathroom and checked the children like I always do—and she's gone!' For a minute, I didn't know who she was talking about, until Mr. Abbott came out of Abby's room and I saw the empty crib.

''Mr. and Mrs. Abbott searched the house like mad people,'' Kezia had said, her eyes sad and focused on the memory. ''Mrs. Abbott kept screaming Abigail's name while Sawyer ran up and down the stairs looking for her, and Daniel and Mr. Abbott searched the grounds. Campbell and I cried.

''Mr. Abbott called the police, but they found no evidence of a break-in. They thought either the laundry chute or the dumbwaiter might have been entry points if someone had gotten into the basement. But the door was still locked from the inside, and none of the windows was broken. They interviewed the staff, thinking, I guess, that one of us might have kidnapped her, but that was preposterous. We all loved the children like our own." Kezia paused and sighed heavily, spreading her hands in a gesture of helplessness. "They even sent the police to get Killian at five-thirty in the morning to see if he remembered seeing anyone around the place, or if any of the many tradesmen who'd worked on a plumbing and carpentry repair problem several weeks earlier had shown a particular interest in Abby. Killian was a sharp little boy and never missed anything. He didn't remember anyone with an interest in his little sister, but he did recall the name of everyone who'd been in the house. Then..." Kezia drew a ragged breath. "I remember him turning to his father and telling him he was sorry he hadn't been home. That if he had been, the kidnapping might not have happened. His father told him not to think that, that *he'd* been home and he hadn't been able to stop it. But Killian was a dedicated big brother, and I think he carries guilt to this day." Kezia swiped a hand across her eyes and went on.

"Then it was as though life in this house just stopped. There were no clues, nothing at all to go on, and the Abbotts just waited and prayed. At that point, they'd have been happy to get a call for ransom, to know that Abigail was alive and could be paid for and brought home again.

"They went on television and begged for her return. They spoke to any reporter who'd listen. And we all waited. No conversation in the house, no laughter and eventually no hope."

"How horrible," Cordie whispered.

Kezia nodded. "Then one day Mrs. Abbott got up, called us all together—husband, kids, staff—and said we weren't going to live this way any longer, that there were three other children to think about and everyone's lives had to move on. We would hold Abigail in our hearts and keep praying, but we were to start living again." Kezia's lips trembled. "I thought it was very brave of her."

"Yes." Cordie wrapped her arms around herself and tried to imagine how she would feel if a child was stolen from her with no evidence of what had happened and no knowledge whether he or she was dead or alive.

"But Kate was devastated, felt responsible and finally quit the following year to go live with her sister in Los Angeles."

"How awful for everyone."

"Yes, it was. Everyone was affected. I think all the boys carry scars from the ordeal. Chloe dedicated herself to her remaining children, but sometimes I see a terrible sadness in her eyes. And Mr. Nathan put on a good front, but Abby was his little girl and he never got over losing her. He died with her name on his lips."

Cordie groaned and put a hand over her eyes as tears welled. What an old and deeply rooted pain for Killian—for all the family. Killian, though, was her primary concern, and wanting to remove his guilt so she could put her love there, instead, would be no easy task.

She wondered now if her initial approach had

been wrong. He was so serious-minded, such a workaholic, that when she'd married him, she'd tried to joke him out of his grave nature, lure him away from work once in a while in the hope that his having a personal life would help him loosen up, open up. But in the end he'd resented her for it.

This time, she had to find another way. Take things more seriously, so that he didn't mistake her for a lightweight. Work as much as he did so that he'd know she wanted success for Abbott Mills as much as he did.

She groaned again and laid a forearm across her eyes, propping her feet on the coffee table. That would be a big job. She generally found life amusing, so she was always joking, pulling pranks. She liked sound and color and gravitated toward those things. That was why she loved fashion and concerts and parties.

Of course, all she had to do was reconsider the status of her relationship with Killian—that put a genuine pall over everything. Working a lot would give her less time to think.

She carried her untouched tray into the kitchen, covered the lasagna with plastic wrap, put it in the refrigerator and left the salad out to pick at.

She should call her parents and let them know how she was. They'd been worried about her when she'd gone to Scotland, and finally flown out from Texas to check on her. They'd been horrified to find her pale and thin and holed up in the lodge like a recluse.

"He isn't worth it," her mother had said firmly. Judith and Gregory Hyatt had loved Killian, though they'd known him only briefly. But Judith had always been her only child's staunchest support system, and though Cordie had been caught in another man's bed, Judith was sure the problem couldn't be with Cordie and therefore Killian had to have misunderstood.

When Cordie had told her parents she was going back to New York to apply for the position of buyer that had miraculously opened up at Abbott Mills, her father had thought her crazy. "Cord, he's furious with you. He's divorcing you. Why give him the chance to deny your application or use it as an excuse to dump all over you again?"

Cordie had shaken her head. "He won't even know about the job until it's time for the quarterly personnel report. The hope is that I'll be so entrenched by the time he notices I'm on board that my immediate superiors will support me."

"She loves him, darling," her mother had tried to explain to her father.

He didn't get it. "You said this divorce was all his fault."

"It is."

"Then why does she love him?"

"Because…the separation is his fault, but the problems he has that are making him do it aren't."

Her father, the CEO of one of the country's finest furniture makers and a millionaire in his own right, though not in the Abbott class, stared dumbly at his wife.

Her mother patted his chest. "It's love, dear. You just don't understand those things. Trust Cordie. She's always known what she's doing."

While she appreciated her mother's confidence in her, she now hoped it wasn't misplaced.

Suddenly, taking a shower and going to bed had it all over eating and spending an evening watching television.

Loving Killian Abbott was exhausting.

Chapter Three

Killian intended to sleep late Saturday morning, but his room was flooded with sunlight at 6:00 a.m. After tossing and turning for an hour, he finally got up, pulled on shorts and a T-shirt and went down to the kitchen and made himself an omelette.

Kezia discovered him as he was buttering toast, her expression horrified. "You fend for yourself all the time," she said, looking with surprise into the frying pan. "When you're home, I'm supposed to cook for you."

He kissed her cheek, scooped his omelette onto the plate that held his toast and headed for the porch. "It's okay," he said over his shoulder. "It's the weekend for you, too. I told Daniel I wouldn't need him until Monday. Don't fuss."

She grumbled further, but he stepped out onto the deck and closed the door behind him. A large lawn sloped to blueberry bushes, then a small apple orchard that sheltered a path to the beach.

He was just beginning to mellow out from a hectic week when again Cordie came to mind. He envisioned her in the back room of her department, her red hair in two French braids looped around the back of her head, giving her a false air of dignity. Her brown eyes had been enormous against her natural redhead's pallor, but they'd had little of the frivolity he remembered from their marriage. She was taller than average, but looked thinner now. Their separation had probably upset her, but he could make no concessions. They weren't compatible. They never had been.

Too bad he hadn't seen that when they'd first met. But he'd been blinded by her glorious hair and her ivory shoulders in a little black dress.

He shook his head against the thought and reminded himself that he was here to relax.

He ate his omelette and made himself count the bank of trees in the distance to prevent himself from thinking of her.

He went to the beach with an old paperback copy of a Robert Parker book and read until he reached a point in the dialogue where the hero and heroine argued about their relationship. Suddenly, his mind was replaying his conversation with Cordie rather than focusing on the dialogue he was reading.

He got to his feet, wondering why a very busy man ever thought his body would allow him to relax for a weekend. It was accustomed to action—albeit corporate action—and his brain was used to making big, quick decisions.

He went back to the house and called Lew Weston, Abbott Mills's troubleshooter and one-man think tank.

"I thought you were taking the weekend off," Lew said.

"I am," Killian replied. "I just wondered if we got that report I asked for on the Florida Shops."

"We got it. It'll wait for you until Monday."

"Your wife wasn't upset that you volunteered to work the weekend?"

"No. I promised her dinner and the theater."

"Smart man."

"Yes, I am. So let me do my job and you get back to the beach or whatever it is you're doing."

Killian hung up and headed for the Vespa Campbell kept in the garage. He took a tour of the acreage. Nothing to find fault with here. Acres of apple trees blossomed in perfectly formed rows all the way up to the trees on the neighboring property. Campbell knew what he was doing.

The roads were bumpy and dusty, but the air smelled of sea grass and salt and held the unmistakable sweetness of early summer. The fragrance filled his being, and for reasons he couldn't explain, seemed to distill itself into the image of Cordie.

With a growl, he rode the bike back to the garage and went into the house to find Kezia fixing dinner despite his insistence that he was self-sufficient. So he went upstairs to take a shower, dressed in fresh slacks and a white cotton sweater and asked the staff to join him for dinner.

Winfield frowned at him. "We know you're a

democratic despot, Mr. Abbott,'' he said politely. ''You don't have to prove it to us.''

He denied that was his point. ''You eat with Mom all the time. She told me.''

''But that's Miss Chloe,'' Daniel said with the same frown Winfield wore. ''You're…you're…''

''The democratic despot?''

''Yes, sir.''

''You used to eat with me when I was a child.''

''No, you ate with us in the kitchen. That was before you became one of the Fortune 500.''

''Then sit down with me or heads will roll.''

They did, but it was dessert before they were comfortable.

He slept in Sunday morning, then took a call from Chloe as he ate breakfast on the deck.

''Tante Bijou isn't at all well,'' she told him, ''and the housekeeper is worried. She wouldn't let her call me. So I've taken over her care and I might be longer than I expected. Is that all right with you?''

''Of course,'' he answered her. ''Stay as long as she needs you.''

''Thank you, Killian. Give my love to Sawyer and Campbell.''

''I will.''

Campbell arrived home Sunday night—by helicopter. It landed in the middle of the front lawn with rotors beating so loudly that the sound brought everyone in the house to the side porch.

As they watched, Campbell leaped to the grass,

ran clear of the rotors, then waved as the 'copter pulled up again and sailed off into the sky, causing a wind storm in the fruit trees and the poplars.

"He didn't get arrested again, did he?" Winfield asked. He held a large free weight in one hand, obviously interrupted in the middle of his evening workout.

"He didn't call us for bail," Killian replied. "And that wasn't a police helicopter."

Kezia used the wooden spoon in her hand to point in the direction the helicopter had taken. "That's his friend Billie Sandusky. She flew him to his interview."

Killian and Winfield both turned to her in interest.

She shrugged. "No, I don't know if they're romantic," she said, apparently eager to fend off their questions. "But I hope not. She drinks straight shots, and I don't like to see that in a woman."

Daniel, standing at the bottom of the stairs with a greasy rag in his hands, warned her with a quiet, "Kezia." He didn't wear a uniform and his manner was easy and friendly, but he was always careful never to overstep his position as an employee in the Abbott household—something that was difficult to do in a relationship as long-standing as theirs.

Kezia, on the other hand, often offered her opinion, and seldom with any deference. But the whole family loved her anyway.

Killian frowned at her. "And how do you know what Billie drinks?"

"I play bridge with her mother's housekeeper.

The girl's out of control, and with Campbell's confusion about who he is and where he belongs, he doesn't need that.'' Then she seemed to realize that was crossing the line, even for her. She cleared her throat. ''Not that that's any of my business. I'll just go back to my cake.''

''Hey, Daniel!'' Campbell slapped Daniel on the shoulder as he loped past him and up the steps.

''Mr. Campbell.'' Daniel shrugged an apology at Killian for his wife's candor and went back to the garage.

Campbell grinned at Killian and Winfield. ''Gentlemen.'' He transferred his grip on his overnight bag to shake hands. ''Winfield. Killer. Nice of you to meet my helicopter. Did you miss me, or is this an attempt to prevent my return?''

Winfield clapped his shoulder. ''Nice to see you back safe and sound, Mr. Campbell.'' Then he took off toward the basement stairs and the gym.

Campbell was dark-featured like Chloe, a few inches shorter than Killian and more slender, though his work on the estate had given him well-developed shoulders and upper arms. Chloe was always telling him that his job was to oversee the temporary help harvesting the apples, but he'd never been one to stand by and watch.

Killian remembered trying to teach him to bat a baseball as children. The lesson had resulted in Campbell's taking the bat from him and swinging until he was exhausted. His father had told Killian that determination was sometimes more important than skill in achieving success.

"Depends," Killian teased in response to Campbell's question, even as he gave him a fraternal shove into the front hall. "Did you take the job?"

"It hasn't been offered to me yet," Campbell replied. "They have six other applicants."

"Do you want it?"

"It's Florida."

Killian shrugged. "Sunshine every day. Funny-tasting tropical fruit. Big deal."

"Women in string bikinis," Campbell countered with a longing look, "all day, every day, all year long. Going to the beach on your coffee break in February, baseball spring-training camps."

"You're only yards from the beach here." That was a flimsy argument and Killian knew it. But there were issues unresolved between the brothers, and he didn't want him hundreds of miles away until they'd fixed them.

Campbell put his bag down near the hall table. "If you went to the beach here in February, you'd be the ice sculpture at Mom's next party." Suddenly he seemed to notice her absence. "She gone already? She left a message on my voice mail saying she was off to Paris with the Mitchells."

"Right. Winfield had fits, but she went anyway. Need a coffee nudge? I've got a pot going in the library."

Campbell studied him suspiciously. "You're not

planning some big heavy conversation about the family, are you?''

The kid had a good brain. "No," Killian lied. "My offer was just an effort to help you relax after your flight."

"Aha!" Campbell pointed a finger at him. "You want to know about Billie!"

Killian shook his head. "I know about Billie. She drinks straight shots and she's out of control. I was just interested in your weekend."

Campbell followed him as he led the way to the library. The room was paneled in warm oak and had floor-to-ceiling bookshelves protected by doors with wire mesh. A ladder on runners provided access to top shelves. Killian and his brothers had terrorized many a nanny on it when they were children. Deep blue upholstered sofas and chairs with an even darker blue stripe were arranged near the fireplace, which now held a pot of flowers.

A granite counter ran along one side of the room as a sort of study area, and Killian, who'd adopted this room as a home office, had installed a bar at one end of it. The aroma of a simple French roast filled that side of the room.

At the far end, Palladian French doors opened out onto the side porch and garden.

Killian poured Kahlúa and brandy in a glass pedestal mug, added coffee, then picked up the drink he'd left there when he'd heard the helicopter. He took them to the sofa where Campbell had settled, handed him his drink, then sat in the chair opposite.

"So, you had time to sightsee?" he asked as Campbell angled one knee over the other and leaned back.

"No," Campbell replied, "but the sights I described are everywhere you look. Definitely one of the perks."

Silence fell. Campbell was waiting for him to ask more questions, and sure his brother would hate that, Killian waited for him to volunteer information.

Campbell sipped his drink, rested the glass on his knee and finally said in a defensive tone, "You know, I wouldn't be abandoning the family if I left here."

Killian nodded calmly. There were only six years between them, but since their father died when Campbell was only seventeen, Killian had taken charge to keep him in school when he'd been offered a job with a software company, to chase him down when he'd run off, to bail him out of jail when he was picked up in a bar brawl in Southhampton. So they had what amounted to father-son issues, though they were brothers and not that far apart in age.

"I know that," Killian said. "And no one's suggesting it."

"Mom is."

"Well, you're her favorite. She'd—"

"No!" Campbell interrupted, grabbing his cup and lowering his foot to the floor in a gesture of impatience. "See! There it is again! That's not true. I'm not her favorite."

Killian raised an eyebrow. "There's what?"

Campbell gestured toward him in clear exaspera-
tion. "That…that suggestion that Mom cares more
about me because I'm her natural son. You act like
I'm the one who's always seeing differences between your half of the family and mine, but you're
the one—"

Killian concentrated on keeping his voice down
as he interrupted. "There are *not* two halves of this
family."

"There are! You don't want to acknowledge it
because you consider yourself the benevolent ruler
of all of us, but we're not the same. You're from the
first line of Abbotts—the founders' circle. Wealth,
position, bloodline. I'm from the second wife, with
none of the above. And when Mom tries to offer
guidance to me, all she talks about is *you!*"

The volume in Killian's voice grew harder to control. "Wealth, position and bloodline did a lot for
Sawyer and me, didn't they?" he demanded. "You
got the mother who stayed!"

Campbell looked taken aback for a moment, then
he said more quietly, "Well, cry me a river. You
got her, too. She didn't give birth to you, but *you're*
her favorite."

Killian shook his head as the absurd words rever-
berated around them. "We sound like a couple of
children. Isn't the important thing that we're all
here?"

Campbell ran a hand over his face and sighed.
"You would think so. But I feel as though I'll never
know who I am as long as I'm here. You're brilliant

in business, Sawyer lives life on the heroic edge and I'm just here—the farmer, the plodder.''

"Campbell…"

"You can deny it all you want, it's still true."

"You're the best estate manager this place has ever had."

"I'm the *only* one it's ever had. You just gave me the job because you got too occupied with the business, and Sawyer has his hands full, what with running the foundation and trying to get himself killed."

"It doesn't matter how you became the estate manager. You are great at it."

Campbell nodded, suddenly calmer. "That's why I think my skills could be marketable elsewhere. If I'm ever going to feel like an Abbott in my own right, I have to do it away from here."

"Away from where the Abbotts *are?*"

Campbell acknowledged with an exasperated nod that that might sound strange. "I know. My life doesn't seem to make sense on any level. I'm just going with my gut."

"Here's something *for* that gut." Sawyer walked into the room with three dessert plates of chocolate cake. Two were splayed in one hand with great dexterity and the third was in the other. He'd been a waiter at the Plucky Duck in town his senior year in high school and every summer in college. Killian remembered that Sawyer's charm had earned him big tips that had helped support his weekend activities when their father had insisted the boys earn their own disposable income so they'd understand what real life was like.

Killian had always considered that the absence of one's natural mother had been a serious dose of real life, but he'd understood his father's point.

Campbell laughed as he reached up to accept his plate. "How do *you* rate?" he asked.

Sawyer handed Killian a plate, then went to sit at the opposite end of the sofa. "I came in through the kitchen. Kezia was just frosting the cake and I turned on my charm."

"Nice of you to share with us." Killian saluted him with his fork. "I remember a time when you'd have absconded with the whole thing and not even worried about us."

"I would have now," he admitted with a grin, "but Kezia said clearly, 'Your brothers are in the library. Two of these are for them.' I wouldn't want to have to answer to her if I didn't share. And I knew you'd blab if I didn't."

"Damn right," Campbell said. "How was *your* trip?"

"Good. A bunch of nice ladies in New Hampshire trying to build a teen shelter with no money. They think if we help them put it up, they can find funding to run the operation."

"Help them?" Killian asked.

"Give them the money," Sawyer clarified.

"Can we do it?"

"With a little artful manipulation."

"*Legal* manipulation?"

''Of course.'' Sawyer replied with wide-eyed innocence, but Killian knew him to be good at that. He told you what you wanted to hear, then went off and did whatever he damn well pleased.

And usually got away with it. He had their mother's straight blond hair, which he currently wore in a spiked style Killian was amazed to find appealed to women. It also stunned boards of directors, who expected to deal with a wild man and found themselves head to head with a savvy street fighter who did everything as though he had nothing to lose.

Sawyer had the same blue eyes Killian had inherited from their father, but his were set in a sophisticated face that didn't look like a Mount Rushmore carving, the way Killian's did.

His smile, too, charmed the ladies, and he had a sense of fun that was hard for anyone to resist. Until he inevitably found the threat in an undertaking and it grew too dangerous for his companions.

He found a way to use that to his advantage by volunteering his daredevil skills every year at the Children with Cancer fund-raiser. Everyone donated eagerly to see what Sawyer would do this year. In the past years, he'd sky-boarded, rappelled the Abbott Building and offered himself at a bachelor auction—less physically arduous but certainly as dangerous.

This year he was waterskiing. Killian wasn't privy to the details, but the stunt didn't sound as harrowing as his previous ones.

Everyone at Shepherd's Knoll worried about him, Killian included—maybe even Killian particularly. They'd been partners in crime as children, support for each other when they couldn't figure out why their mother didn't like them, and they'd decided together to like Campbell when he was born, then to adore Abby.

But something had changed in Sawyer when Abby was taken. Killian was aware of the subtle difference, the slight pulling away, because he himself had been desperately trying *not* to change. Yet the small distance had happened and there'd been nothing he could do about it.

They'd grown to adulthood with a tight fraternal bond, though they'd gone on completely different roads.

"Good," Killian said. "Because bailing out Campbell for brawling is one thing. Pleading your case before the Federal Trade Commission would be something else."

Campbell laughed.

Sawyer glowered at his younger brother. "I thought you and I were allied when it came to standing against Killer's stuffy big-brothering."

"We are," Campbell replied, spearing a large bite of cake. "Unless he's really trashing you, then I kind of enjoy that."

Sawyer sighed. "Tell me you got the job and you're moving soon."

Campbell shook his head while he chewed. "Sorry," he said finally. "You're going to be cursed with me for a little while yet. A few other candidates are under consideration and I'm sure there'll be a second round of interviews.''

Sawyer pretended a long-suffering sigh. ''I've been trying to get rid of you for thirty plus years. I guess I can wait a little longer.''

Campbell shrugged, forking another bite. ''Sorry to make it hard for you, but Killer's working against you.''

Now Sawyer pretended disgust. ''You're not encouraging him to *stay?*'' he asked Killian. ''Come on, this is our chance! We've been plotting it our whole lives.''

''Yeah, but Mom's gone and I'm going to make him host the Women of Losthampton Historical Society. If he leaves, it'll have to be one of us.'' The small-and-aged group met in the house's great room once a month, a perk Chloe had granted them when she joined many years ago.

Sawyer nodded. ''I missed that completely.''

Sawyer and Campbell also had a rapport that didn't involve Killian. Being younger, they'd supported each other's resentments of privileges and attitudes enjoyed by the eldest sibling. So if Killian had any concerns that Campbell would be offended by Sawyer's teasing, they were laid to rest by Campbell's grim expression as he caught chocolate crumbs—all that was left on his plate—with the flat edge of his fork. The look was completely false and there was laughter in his eyes.

''The ladies like me better than either of you, anyway," Campbell said, getting to his feet. "Four or five of them have me lined up for their daughters."

Sawyer smiled at Killian. "That could work. We'd still get rid of him." Then he looked puzzled. "I thought Mom was just gone for the weekend."

"Tante Bijou's under the weather. She's staying to take care of her for a while. She sends both of you her love."

"Well, you're getting rid of me right now." Campbell stretched and Sawyer moved his head aside theatrically, evading the fork in his right hand. "Selling my good qualities has been more exhausting than I realized."

"Mmm," Sawyer said. "All that stuff you had to make up, probably." He had to shout the last few words as Campbell left the room.

Sawyer stood up to pour himself a cup of coffee, then sat down again and picked up his cake. "Does he think he aced the interview?" he asked Killian, suddenly seriously.

Killian shrugged. "He didn't say. He got defensive about why he wanted to leave, and I tried to tell him he was valuable here, and we got into it like we always do. So, I don't know."

Sawyer nodded, familiar with Campbell's attitude. "He just needs to get away and realize we don't make him feel he doesn't belong—he does it to himself."

Killian couldn't help a laugh. "You just told him we've been plotting to get rid of him for years."

Sawyer laughed, too. "Yeah. But he knows I'm kidding. Doesn't he?"

"I'm sure he does."

"What'd the two of you fight about?"

Killian said intrepidly, "Which one of us Mom loves the most."

Sawyer made a scornful noise. "That's easy. Me."

KILLIAN RODE to work Monday morning in the back seat of the limo, checking stock-market quotes on his laptop, grateful that his calendar showed a relatively easy day. He'd had a good weekend, but he feared he was losing what little ability he had to relax. Not that he understood why he was worried about it. He'd been a workaholic since college, when his father had given him a part-time job keeping statistics on production costs for every business within the corporation, sales figures and every other recordable process in between.

Once in the city, he thanked Daniel and wished him a good day, then took his private elevator to the twenty-third floor. He responded with a smile to all the polite "Good morning, Mr. Abbott's" directed at him. His mail was on his desk, along with a steaming cup of coffee and a brioche Barbara had bought from the Montmartre Bakery on her way in from the subway.

Life was good at the office, he thought as he remembered his pleasant but very quiet weekend at home. There, he'd had to work to fill the time. Of course, Chloe had been gone, and his brothers hadn't returned until Sunday night. But was he so unused to his own company that he was now lonely by himself?

The notion surprised him.

He took a sip of coffee, bit into the freshly baked roll and went through the mail and e-mail messages.

He noticed a memo from human resources, asking him to call Jack regarding the sudden revelation of confidential information about an employee. He was about to put the memo aside until after he'd handled a few things he thought had priority, when he saw that the employee in question was Cordelia Magnolia Hyatt.

He called Jack.

CORDIE READ the current issue of *InStyle* while eating a bagel and drinking a cup of tea at a little deli across the street from Abbott's. She'd worked all day Sunday, taking advantage of the quiet of the closed store to put out new stock and fill a sales rack, so she could afford a few moments to herself this morning. The staff knew where she was if there was a problem.

Not that she was enjoying her solitude. The sesame-and-asiago bagel that had looked so appealing when she'd ordered it didn't want to go down, and she was having second thoughts about her decision to work at Abbott's and try to reclaim her marriage. The idea had seemed like such a good one, until she'd come face-to-face with Killian's hostility on

Friday. In her absence from him, she'd managed to forget how completely disgusted he'd been with her when he'd found her in Brian's bed, and how serious he'd been when he'd told her their marriage was over.

She tried to brace herself with a sip of peppermint tea. "Come on," she told herself. "You knew this would be hard. Did you think the circumstances were going to change and make it easier for you just because you dreamed of Killian welcoming you back with open arms? You knew there was no real chance of that. You analyzed this from all angles and decided you loved him enough to try it. Buck up! You're not going to weasel out at the first roadblock. You're just discouraged because you feel a little puny this morning."

She took another sip of tea.

Her mind in a muddle, she didn't even notice Killian walk into the deli until he stood directly across from her.

His eyes were dark but unreadable. She didn't quite see anger in their depths, but some other black emotion she couldn't analyze.

"You're pregnant," he said in a tone that was more of an accusation than an announcement.

She closed her eyes and accepted that this day was not going to improve anytime soon.

When they'd gotten married, she'd fantasized about announcing a pregnancy to him one day, but in her dreams that moment had never taken place in a deli buzzing with conversation. And he'd been proud and happy, not…whatever that dark look was in his eye.

He took the chair opposite her.

"How far along are you?" he asked tersely.

She knew what the question really asked. "Yes, it's your baby," she replied. "Even if you don't believe me, the hotel incident was three months ago and I'm four months along. I can provide proof, if that's necessary."

"It isn't necessary. The report from your doctor said so."

"But that's not why I'm back. I don't have some plan to prove your paternity and secure an Abbott inheritance for him or her. I just want to work, I love fashion retail and Abbott's is the best there is." She drew a breath and made herself look him in the eye. His dark expression was darkening further, but she refused to be intimidated. "You were pretty clear the other day about any hope of reconciliation, so I've given up on that." She willed herself to appear clear-eyed and honest rather than like the big fat liar she really was. "But I want to keep the job."

He met her gaze unflinchingly. She wondered if those blue eyes saw beyond her pretense. She couldn't be sure. And she couldn't tell how he felt about the news that she was carrying his baby. He might be angry only at her and not the pregnancy.

"You've seen a doctor?" he asked.

"Of course. One in Scotland, then Dr. Rosenkrantz on Tenth Street when I came here. She says I'm fine."

He didn't seem to believe that. "You're pale and thin."

"I've had a major battle with morning sickness, but I'll get over it."

"Jack Eagan," he said quietly, his voice losing its edge of anger, "is worried about you handling heavy stock. And your staff said you worked Sunday to put the new lines out."

"It's easier when there's no one around."

He acknowledged that with a nod. "But wrestling with heavy boxes when there's no one around to help you isn't smart."

Tension rose and stretched between them. Or maybe it was just within her. He sounded worried about her. He was even more controlled than usual, and she wondered if that was some effort he made to prevent himself from shouting recriminations at her.

"I'll be more careful," she promised, reaching for her teacup, then changing her mind. She pushed the cup away.

He noticed the gesture.

She tried to distract him with a frontal attack. "Did you come here to fire me?"

"I could." His forehead pleated when he studied her face. "You lied on your application."

"It didn't ask if I was pregnant," she argued.

"But it did ask you to apprise the company of any medical condition we should know about. I shouldn't have to hear about it from Jack when he noticed the doctor put restrictions on your lifting, then read your physical report in detail to find out why.''

She shook her head. ''The company doesn't have to know about my pregnancy. It's personal.''

He rolled his eyes over the obvious. ''And how long did you expect to be able to keep it a secret?''

She ignored that. It was all part of the plan. ''You said you wanted nothing to do with me. I presumed you'd just stay away from me.''

''That's wrong on several levels,'' he corrected mildly. ''Pregnancy is a condition the company should know about in order to ensure your safety on the job. And your pregnancy was something I should have known about as the baby's father.''

She stiffened. ''I wasn't going to use the baby to get you back.'' Her conscience whispered, *Liar! Liar!*

''You were using it to keep me away,'' he argued. ''You knew if you told me about the baby, I'd want to be involved.''

She'd prayed that was how he'd feel. But he couldn't know that.

''I don't want you involved,'' she lied again. *Pants on fire!*

''That's too bad.'' He frowned at her bagel, with the single bite out of it, and the cup of tea she'd pushed away. ''You finished with those?''

''Yes.''

He got to his feet and came around to help her out of her chair. ''Okay,'' he said, holding out the pink silk jacket that matched her pants. ''Let's go get your things.''

She ignored the jacket and turned to him in alarm. "I thought you weren't firing me."

"Not your work things." He walked around her to force her arms into the sleeves. "Your personal things. You're moving into Shepherd's Knoll until the baby comes. I've already told your staff not to expect you back today."

"What?" she demanded, turning to face him again, one arm in the sleeve of her jacket. That was precisely what she wanted, but he couldn't know that, either.

"It's a compromise between our different points of view. You don't want me involved, but I want to be."

"If I move into your home?' she asked, gesturing with the empty sleeve. The end of her jacket swung in a wide arc and knocked the newspaper out of the hands of a man at the counter. "I'm so sorry," she said, handing the paper back to him. Then she demanded more quietly of Killian, "How is that a compromise for *you?*"

"I didn't fire you, did I?" He put her other arm in the sleeve, handed her her purse and magazine, then pushed her gently toward the door.

She stopped him in the middle of the sidewalk. He put his hands in his pockets and drew a sigh, probably for patience.

"We have to settle something," she insisted.

"What's that?"

"Your point in doing this." She had to make this look convincing. "What do you expect to gain?"

"The baby," he said, without even stopping to think.

She blinked at him, a little ripple of panic in the pit of her stomach making her completely forget the now *not-so-clever* plan. "What?"

"The baby," he repeated. "It's an Abbott. Mine."

She had a horrible feeling she understood what he meant, but she had to be sure. "You said you didn't want to reconcile."

"That's right," he said.

She folded her arms so he wouldn't see her hands tremble. "You're planning to keep me at Shepherd's Knoll," she said, her voice a victim of the same trembling, "until the baby's born, then take it away from me?"

"We'll work out a deal."

Without a second thought, she struck him hard in the shoulder. "You don't *deal* over a baby!" To herself, she added, "This isn't part of my plot! You're supposed to just invite me back into your life, then we learn to love each other again and become a family."

"I'm not giving up my claim to the baby," Killian said unequivocally.

"It's mine!"

"It's ours. And trying to pretend I don't figure in his life isn't going to work. So we *have* to deal."

She was suddenly aware that her "plot" had a serious pitfall she hadn't considered. If she couldn't get Killian back, he was going to fight her for the baby—and he had an army of brilliant lawyers.

"You're hateful!" she said in a heartfelt whisper.

He gave her a brief nod as though that was of no consequence. "I gathered you felt that way when you slept with Brian."

Chapter Four

Killian smiled wryly at Cordie's wardrobe closet. It was stuffed with clothing, two racks of shoes, a tie rack that she used for belts and scarves and a shelf of purses. "When do you wear all this?" he asked.

"I have a very active social life," she replied with a disdainful glance in his direction. "When you're always at the office, always in a board meeting, always traveling to acquire more businesses and therefore meeting with other workaholics, all you need is the same suit in a few different colors." Her eyes went from the shoulder of his beige Armani jacket to where the hem of the slacks broke over his John Lobb shoes. "Those of us who actually have a life need different things to wear for different occasions."

He reached into the closet to catch the sleeve of something familiar. It was a glittery vanilla-colored dress with a low back, which she'd bought on their honeymoon in Florence. He remembered that she'd brushed her hair down that night, but she'd worn it caught back at the sides with a pair of diamond-studded silver barrettes he'd purchased for her that afternoon.

They'd had dinner at the Hostaria del Bricco, walked within the walls of the ancient city of Florence, then made love all night long and most of the following day.

He felt a rush of emotion at the memory of the complete adoration he'd felt for her, the stunning realization that she loved him with her entire being. He'd felt superior and elated because of the way her look and her touch affected him.

His brother's and his staff called him Killer, and not just because it was an easy nickname for Killian. He could outlast anyone in negotiations, stand firm well after exhaustion and ill temper had claimed everyone else. He was known for thinking clearly and unsentimentally when everyone else had given up, and for seldom being wrong.

So he'd been as shocked as anyone when he'd fallen like an anvil for the breathtakingly beautiful, always laughing prankster-at-heart Cordelia Hyatt.

Sawyer had thought she was after Killian's money, and denied that it mattered that her father was a millionaire and that she'd had a successful modeling career before giving it up to become a buyer for Bloomford's department stores. "He has *one* million," Sawyer pointed out. "A lot of people do nowadays. To have status in society around here, you have to have your millions in multiples. Yours are in the hundreds."

"So are yours."

"Yes, thanks to you. But she's after you, not me."

Sawyer had been coolly polite to her in the beginning, but was finally won over like everyone else. Her good cheer and her beauty were irresistible.

Then he'd finally been proved wrong after the Brian debacle when Killian had asked her to leave. She'd pleaded with him to listen to her explanation one more time, but her insistence that Brian had forced his way to her bed when she'd been in *his* room, hadn't seemed like much of an explanation and he'd refused.

He'd offered her a substantial seven figures to go quickly and without fuss. She'd hit him with a very large leather purse and left without the check. When he'd deposited it into her account, she'd couriered a check back to him in a box with her wedding ring, the diamond combs—and a male rag doll stuck with pins. He could only conclude that was her version of a voodoo curse.

He'd stuffed the doll behind a box of personal papers he kept on a top shelf in his wardrobe closet. He wasn't sure why he hadn't thrown it away, except that he suspected she'd made the doll herself, and with its many pins piercing it, it looked precisely the way he'd felt for years—except for the first month or so he'd been married to her. Until he'd begun to wake up from his lovesick stupor and wonder what he'd done. Until he'd realized she was all about laughter and silliness, and he…wasn't.

He was heir to a fortune, and to a tragedy that

had changed his family forever. He didn't have time
to laugh.

He came back to awareness, realizing that he held
the hem of a sleeve of the honeymoon dress in his
fingers and Cordie was watching him. Time stopped
and grew heavy for a moment as they stared at each
other—she, probably remembering that night as he
did. Her dark eyes grew large and sad, then she drew
in a breath and slapped the sleeve out of his hand.

"That doesn't fit me anymore," she said, taking
a simple pale green jumper several hangers over.
"I'm not showing very much yet, but only things
with a loose waist still fit."

She yanked a dress bag out of the corner of the
closet and slipped it over the clothes she'd chosen
while he held the hangers.

After pulling shoes out of a rack on the side of
her closet she tossed them into an open bag on the
bed. She stuffed undies and stockings into a beach
bag, then went into the bathroom, where he heard
the clink of bottles and jars.

She emerged with a train case he remembered
from their honeymoon and added it to the pile in the
middle of the bed.

"Now," she said, looking around her, "I just have
to find Versace."

"Who?"

"My cat."

"Cordie, I'm not sure…"

"One of his favorite spots," she said, ignoring his
protest, her tone distracted as she got down on her

hands and knees at the edge of the closet, "is…on top of my…sweats. Sachi? Sachi!"

He was about to tell her there'd never been a cat at Shepherd's Knoll, but the tantalizing view of her tight backside in the silky pants distracted him from his intention. Though she was all wrong for him, she was a masterpiece of nature—full bosom, slender waist, nicely rounded but muscled hips, long, lean legs.

Desire stirred in him, hot and, at the moment at least, unwelcome.

"Hi, Sachi!" Cordie's voice changed suddenly to a croon. "Come here. Come on. We're going to go for a ride. Yes, I know you don't like that, but…" She wriggled slightly backward and raised her head, her arms still invisible under the clothes. "Killy, there's a cat carrier on the shelf above me. See it?"

He reached up to a small gray plastic box with a barred door—like a little prison. He brought down the carrier. "Got it."

"Put it on its side," she directed, "so that the door is uppermost."

He did that.

"Okay. We're going to get one shot at this because he hates the carrier. Open it and I'm going to drop him in. If he sees what I'm doing, he's going to be gone."

"Okay." Killian closed the bedroom door, then braced himself for action as Cordie came backward out of the closet, something in her arms that was fuzzy and gray and far too big to be a cat.

The creature lay docilely in her arms while she got to her feet, then he turned his head in Killian's direction, and a pair of suspicious green eyes locked with his. Cordie took a step toward the carrier, while Killian stood by, the cat's eyes still on him.

As he watched, he saw the expression in the animal's eyes change from suspicion to an awareness of danger. Two front paws stiffened against Cordie's chest.

Killian, remembering the feel of the soft ivory silk breasts in his hands and their vulnerability to those sturdy claws, made a move toward her—and that was a fatal mistake.

With a shriek of displeasure, the cat skittered over her shoulder, onto the bed, then into the bathroom.

"Now you've scared him!" Cordie accused Killian as she took off in pursuit, her hair disheveled and her elegant white shirt puckered and pierced by the cat's claws. "Sachi? Where are you, Sachi?"

A good twenty minutes went by before Killian caught the cat's right rear leg under a reproduction ball-and-claw bathtub elegantly mounted in a sort of steel cradle.

"Get the box!" he shouted at Cordie.

"You're going to break his leg!" she protested.

He was on his stomach on the floor, his ruined suit jacket discarded after a long and torturous chase through the bathroom, back into the bedroom and into the bathroom again. He'd been under the tub, behind the john, in the closet and under the bed, and he was in no mood to be accused of animal abuse.

As far as he was concerned, this cursed cat could be left in the apartment to starve.

"I am holding on to the wrong end of a chain saw," he said with measured patience as teeth and claws ripped into his hand and forearm to the music of demonic screams. "Get the damn box."

In a moment the box was slammed down on the floor beside him. He hauled the cat out with great resolve, held him firmly despite the teeth in his knuckles and tried to drop him into the carrier.

As determined to stay out of the box as Killian was to get him in, the cat flailed the air with his hind legs, pushed them against the box, straddled the opening, then tried to remove Killian's appendix with them.

Cordie finally took firm hold of them, shouted, "Now!" and forced the cat into the carrier and closed and latched the door.

Breathing heavily, they sat on the bathroom floor on either side of the box while it rattled and shook and exuded Versace's high-pitched displeasure.

"This is a pet?" Killian asked. "Kept for the purposes of comfort and companionship?"

Cordie smiled wryly back. "I keep him because he reminds me of my life with you."

CORDIE HAD BEEN WORRIED about how she'd be received at Shepherd's Knoll. She'd left under a cloud of infidelity, and the Abbotts were a tight family with a loyal staff. Despite her denial of such behavior, Killian obviously believed it, and she presumed everyone else did, too.

But Daniel drove them to Losthampton full of questions about how she'd been and telling her about Kezia's sixtieth birthday celebration with family and friends, and the latest grandchild, a boy, who'd been born in May.

In the few months of her marriage to Killian, Cordie had appreciated that the staff were indulged almost as much as the family. Even now, Killian made no attempt to remind his chauffeur that the situation was fairly delicate and his chatty questions for the woman who'd purportedly cheated on his employer and was now being divorced by him might not be appropriate. He simply sat back, watched the dunes and beach grass go by and let them talk.

When they turned onto the poplar-lined driveway that led to Shepherd's Knoll, Cordie grew tense. Daniel was by nature a sweet and caring man; his kindness was one thing. But she had to be prepared for the rest of the household to be more judgmental.

She watched the grand late-1800s house grow larger. Her favorite detail of it had always been the Queen Anne–style circular side porch on the towerlike side of the house. The second-floor bedroom, though unfinished when she'd lived there, always made her feel as though she stood in a turret.

As they approached, her fear about how the household would accept her increased. Then the big double doors flew open and people streamed out of the house and down the steps to the car. Daniel braked smoothly.

"I thought you promised me you wouldn't tell the family until I could," Killian said, unlocking his door. His tone was less accusatory than accepting.

Daniel raised both hands, palms up. "I had to tell Kezia so she could have a room ready. You can probably blame your brothers and Winfield knowing on her."

Kezia was first in line to greet Cordie as Killian stepped out of the limo and offered her a hand.

"Mrs. Abbott!" Kezia exclaimed, wrapping her arms around her. They'd been good friends while Cordie had lived at Shepherd's Knoll. "It's so nice to have you back. I put you in the turret room."

Cordie was thrilled—by Kezia's warm reception *and* her assignment to the turret room. It had windows all around and a full balcony, and summer was just the season to enjoy it. Chloe had been in the process of redecorating it in soft pastels and casual prints and Cordie had watched the progress in fascination.

Now she would live in the room for five months or so. The only thing better would be sharing Killian's room, but she knew that was out of the question.

Sawyer scooped her up into his arms and swung her full circle, while Daniel and Kezia laughed. She clung to his neck with a little scream of alarm until he set her on her feet again and hugged her.

"Good to see you, sis. You look…um…"

There'd been a compliment on the tip of his tongue, but as he'd scrutinized her he'd probably noticed her pallor and her unkempt state after the battle with Versace.

"You look great!" Campbell elbowed Sawyer aside and wrapped his arms around her. "Kezia's going to plump you up in no time. And being around us will put the sparkle back in your eyes. That is, if we keep Killer out of your way. He's enough to put a worried expression on anybody's face."

"Thank you, Campbell," Killian said with obvious irony. He reached into the car, retrieved the cat carrier and handed it to his youngest brother. "It would be nice of you to carry Versace up to Cordie's room for her."

The cat hissed and snarled and the box moved violently as Killian held it by the handle. Everyone took several steps back.

Sawyer, whom Cordie remembered was fearless and always needed to prove it, stepped forward to take the carrier. "What is it?" he asked as the box moved violently again in the transfer of hands.

"It's just a cat," Cordie said, rubbing her fingers gently over the door. The cat responded with a hiss and a snarl. "He's traumatized by the cage, that's all, and the fact that we had to chase him all over the place to catch him and put him inside. He's really very sweet."

"He looks like a killer," Sawyer observed.

"Mmm," Campbell concurred. Then, with a glance at Killian, he added significantly, "I'm surprised you didn't name him that. I see clear similarities.''

Winfield went to take her bags out of the limo, but Campbell stopped him. ''I'll do that,'' he said.

Unhappy at having nothing else to do but greet Cordie, Winfield came forward with a stern expression and offered his hand. ''Welcome back, Mrs. Abbott,'' he said.

Ah. She recognized him as the one holdout against a real welcome. But she didn't blame him. She knew the Abbotts' security and safety were his primary concerns and anything that threatened those—personally as well as physically—he considered a danger to the family.

She shook his hand and smiled in the face of his grimness. ''Thank you, Winfield. It's good to see you again.''

''Thank you, ma'am.'' Not ''Good to see you, too.'' Well, she couldn't blame him. Only time would tell if forcing her way back into Killian's life had been a stroke of genius or a disaster of titanic proportions.

Killian excused himself to make a phone call, and Cordie joined a small parade led by a chattering Kezia. Sawyer followed with the yowling cat, and Campbell brought up the rear with Cordie's dress bag over his arm and her other bags caught in one hand. She tried to help him, but he insisted that she shouldn't.

''We know you're—'' He stopped abruptly, looking very uncomfortable. Sawyer frowned at him over his shoulder.

She stopped Campbell midstair and took the beach bag and the train case from him. "I'm pregnant. You can say it. Pregnant. And it isn't going to hurt me to carry two small bags. You're both about to be uncles whether you like it or not, so we should just get it all out there where we can talk about it and not give one another furtive glances, wondering what to say."

If she had hoped her candor would open a door on conversation, she was sadly mistaken. They continued their procession up the stairs and into the circular room Cordie had fallen in love with when Killian had brought her home for Labor Day weekend last year.

By then, the room had a new ceiling, and new plaster was being applied to the walls. It had been empty of furniture, and canvas tarps lay everywhere. The air had smelled of that curious yeasty quality of fresh plaster.

"When I was little," Killian had confided as they'd gone to the windows, "I used to think that if I looked hard enough, I could see London." Beyond the windows lay sand, sea grass and a vast ocean.

She'd snuggled her way into his arm. "Why London?" she'd asked. "That's an odd spot for a little boy to imagine from his window. Why not Tortuga? Or Egypt?"

"London is where my mother went when she left us," he'd replied. "The chauffeur was from there.

Anyway, I swore that sometimes at night I could see the lights of London. Until I mentioned it to my father and he came to watch with me and pointed out that what I saw were the lights of a freighter.''

She'd put an arm around his waist and leaned into him. ''I'm sorry,'' she'd whispered, surprised to learn that this tall, kind but serious business genius that she'd met only two weeks earlier at the fashion show had any vulnerabilities whatsoever. He seemed always so in charge of the moment, like the director of events rather than a player.

''Don't be,'' he'd said, shrugging off the momentary nostalgia. ''I have everything anyone could reasonably want.''

''But you're you,'' she'd pointed out. ''An individual. And sometimes what you want might not make sense to everybody else. You can still want your natural mother, even though you have Chloe and everything else.''

He'd raised an eyebrow in surprise, as though he were unaccustomed to being understood. He'd squeezed her to him, and they'd stood at the window for a long time.

Now the room was finished, a pale blue-and-white stripe on the walls giving the space a sort of cabana look. A French Empire bedroom set filled the fairly large room, and a floral blue, pink and white spread covered the bed. A desk and chair stood at the windows, which were bare except for shades that could be pulled down when the sun grew too warm.

The view of the ocean beyond the dunes and sea grass was breathtaking.

Sawyer held up the cat carrier, obviously wondering what to do with it. Kezia indicated an open door that led to a small but elegant full bath. "Put it down in there," she suggested, "and let him get acquainted."

"Okay," Sawyer said, placing the carrier on the bathroom's pale blue carpeting. "But I'm not opening the door."

Cordie rolled her eyes at him and elbowed him aside good-naturedly as she went to do it. "When I was here last, you were sky-boarding for entertainment. Don't tell me you're afraid of a little cat."

"Little? That cat weighs thirty pounds if he weighs an ounce. Falling to my death is one thing, but being peeled like an orange by those claws is another."

She put a hand to his chest and pushed him backward toward the door. "Then get out of range, because I'm going to loose the great big scary monster."

Versace suspiciously eyed the open door, sniffed the air with a blotchy pink-and-black nose, then settled back into the carrier, apparently determined to remain in it for the time being. But not without snarling his annoyance.

Cordie closed the bathroom door, certain he'd investigate when he felt comfortable.

"I'll get him some chicken," Kezia said, opening the French doors that led onto the patio. "Let some air in here so the room doesn't smell so new. Lunch will be ready in fifteen minutes. As I recall, you like my chicken-and-pasta salad.''

Cordie remembered that it was wonderful, but wondered whether she'd be able to eat it. ''Maybe I'll just skip lunch, if that's all right,'' she said. ''I'll put my things away and—''

''You can't do that,'' Killian said from the doorway. ''You didn't have breakfast. You'll starve if you don't have something.''

Kezia read the situation. ''Bad morning sickness?''

Cordie nodded.

''What about some fruit?'' Kezia suggested. ''Or I'll make you some custard. We'll just keep trying things until we find something.'' She smiled and patted Cordie's arm. ''Don't worry. That part will be over soon. Then all you'll have to worry about is finding something to wear that fits, locating all the bathrooms wherever you go, charming someone into tying your shoes!''

Killian stepped into the room as Kezia passed him. ''You staying for lunch, Mr. Abbott?'' she asked.

He glanced at his watch and shook his head. ''I have a meeting at two. But I will be home for dinner.''

Everyone turned to him in surprise.

''What?'' he asked, looking from one stunned face to the other. ''I do live here.''

''Usually just on the occasional weekend,''

Campbell replied. He'd placed Cordie's things in the middle of the bed. "You mean we're going to have to put up with you *every* day?" He asked Sawyer with a straight face, "Can we do that?"

"Hopefully, he'll be locked in the library," Sawyer replied. Then he asked Killian gravely, "You're not going to butt into foundation stuff or the running of the estate, are you?"

"I just might." Cordie knew he was teasing. He trusted them completely. Though he kept an eye on them personally and was ready to step in anytime he was needed, he didn't consider them at all inferior because they were younger or because he ran the company that supported the foundation and the estate. "It's time somebody really looked into what you two do all day."

Campbell raised his eyes in supplication. "Please," he murmured as he moved toward the door. "I need the job in Florida more quickly than I'd anticipated."

Sawyer looked heavenward and followed Campbell. "And you can just take me now."

Killian laughed. "I don't think God wants you, Sawyer. In fact, I think he had plans to send you south." He pointed downward, then closed the door.

Cordie smiled fondly at the spot where they'd stood. "I've missed them and their nonsense. I wonder if you have any idea how lucky you are to have siblings."

As soon as the words were out of her mouth, she regretted them. He didn't have *all* of them. She opened her mouth to apologize for her careless choice of words.

He shook his head at her and stepped aside as she pushed open her wardrobe door. It was deep, with a built-in shoe rack, a short rod for tops, a wide one for dresses and coats and a mirror in one corner with hooks for hats.

"Why do you always feel you have to apologize for saying anything that might refer to Abby?" he asked. "Her disappearance was horrible, but we've all learned to deal with it."

She knew he hadn't, or if he had, he'd made some unhealthy sort of adjustment in which he assumed full responsibility.

But sunshine was flooding the room—she was here against all odds—and she didn't want to do anything to challenge this new positive note in her life, however fragile it was.

"I guess it just seems impossible to me that such a thing could ever be dealt with." She smiled at him as she went to the bed, pulled the dress bag toward her and unzipped it. "Don't feel you have to stay around. I have everything I need, so you go on back to your meeting."

She carried a jumper, a dress and a pair of slacks to the closet, but he made no effort to leave. The clothes hung up, she turned to find him watching her with a measuring look.

"What?" she asked, going to the bed to get a light jacket and a few more shirts.

"You understand," he asked, hands in his pockets, "that you're here for the good health of the baby and nothing more?"

As though he hadn't made that abundantly clear. She felt a flash of annoyance and had difficulty suppressing it. She carried the clothes to the closet.

"Not for my seductive body, my enslaving personality and your adoration of me? Yes, I got that." She hung up those clothes, then turned back to him, certain that flare of temper was visible in her eyes.

He noted it, then tipped his head slightly back as though placing himself above the situation. "I just didn't want you to misinterpret the family's welcome as anything—"

"You might feel?" she interrupted, going toward him. He watched her warily, and she knew that despite his pretense of emotional distance, he didn't want her to touch him. And that could only mean he feared she might. And why else would he fear it, unless he was unsure of his own reaction?

"I haven't misinterpreted anything," she said, stopping so close to him that if either of them exhaled, they would touch. His blue eyes never left her face, their gaze steady, even issuing a silent warning. But she'd staked everything on this plot to save her marriage and she intended to stand firm. "You're completely unaffected by what goes on around you, or what anyone else thinks. At least, that's what you'd have us all believe. But I've slept in your arms, remember, during that first month of our marriage that was like a period out of time with the rest of your life. You were open, then. Honest. Not hiding anything. Not hiding *behind* anything.''

He shifted his weight, careful not to touch her. Before he could speak, she plunged on. ''And then you turned off, shutting out something. Protecting yourself from something. And since you fear nothing else…'' Still careful not to touch him, she leaned her head toward him, jutting her chin out in challenge. ''I can only conclude that you're afraid of *me*.''

In a move so quick she didn't see it coming, he opened his hand against her rib cage, fingers spanning her waist as he pushed her gently backward toward the bed.

''Afraid of you?'' he asked, his voice low, dangerous, allowing her a way out if she wanted to give this whole thing a second thought.

But she didn't. She knew what she was doing. She hoped.

''Yes,'' she insisted, letting her voice draw the S out like a sizzle as she stepped back. ''Afraid of *me*.''

She landed on the mattress with a bounce and a little scream of surprise. The beach bag came unbalanced and fell on her face. He brushed it away from her with a sweep of his arm.

POISED OVER HER on his hands and one knee, one foot still braced on the floor, Killian wondered what in the hell he was doing.

He knew what *she* was doing. Her mission here

was either to lure him back into her life, or make him pay for pitching her out of it after he'd found her with Brian. Neither was going to happen, though this was pretty close to the making-him-pay option.

Already disheveled from her feeling ill and chasing the cat, her wild hair escaped its loose confinement and spread around her like a cloud on fire. Nice analogy, he thought absently, for a man who felt he had a foot in hell when he was near her.

To exaggerate the problem, her dark eyes were wide and wary, her lips parted in surprise, her bosom heaving with the sudden activity and probably a suggestion of fear. Or was that desire? He didn't want to see either.

"Afraid of you?" he asked. "You don't seem to present much of a threat, lying on your back."

She smiled thinly. "I think that's where I was most dangerous to you. You forgot yourself when you were making love to me. You could be happy, put aside the fact that your mother cared so little that she left and that Abby disappeared. I let you out of purgatory."

"Consigning me to hell," he argued, "wasn't doing me much of a favor."

"Brian came into *my* room," she insisted quietly. He caught a glimpse of pain in her eyes and attributed it to his unwillingness to fall for the story.

"And you just lie there?" he taunted.

"I was startled." She propped herself up on her elbow, putting their faces just an inch apart. "I was…I'd been asleep. The room had been his. He had another key."

"It doesn't matter." He interrupted her earnest denial. "We're not good together. It's over. I just want to make sure you understand that."

She closed her eyes. Her lips trembled uncertainly and he thought she was going to cry, but she drew a breath that swelled her breast against his chest for one agonizing second. Then she opened her eyes again and looked into his with pity. "I'm carrying your baby. It'll never be as over as you want it to be."

He knew she was right about that. For the rest of their lives there'd be shared custody that would require them to be in touch, to work out amicable arrangements so that the child didn't suffer.

He pushed himself backward until he was on his feet again. "Maybe I'll just sue for full custody."

She bounced up right in front of him, a warrior replacing the seductress of a moment ago.

"Don't threaten me, Killian," she warned. "You may have a courtroom full of brilliant attorneys, but I'm still the baby's mother. All a judge has to hear is that you work twenty-two hours a day, to dismiss your suit without consideration."

"Or that you sleep around to deny your claims to custody," he countered. "Fathers have a lot more rights than they used to have. And I'll claim every one."

"Just to retaliate?" she demanded.

"I don't have time for that kind of pettiness," he assured her. "I'll do it to get the baby."

He watched a succession of strange reactions move across her face—surprise; something that he swore looked like pleasure, though he couldn't imagine why; confusion; then real fear.

"So, you just brought me here to torture me with threats to take the baby?" she finally whispered.

"I brought you here," he replied patiently, "because it matters to me that you're pregnant."

"Because of the baby." It wasn't a question. She seemed convinced that was the case.

He would have simplified his life at that point if he'd just said yes, and immediately. But he was accustomed to honesty in business and in his personal affairs, and at the moment he was a giant knot of raw libido and sincere confusion.

The day he'd opened Brian's hotel-room door to find her in the bed, Brian leaning over her, a clawed hand had ripped out his insides. He'd been certain he could never be sympathetic toward her again.

But he couldn't help being affected by the fact that she already loved his baby so much that she'd become a tigress when he talked about seeking full custody. How beautiful she was, how soft and supple and full of surprises.

He had to remind himself that he didn't want to deal with surprises. That had been a lot of their problem. Where he was concerned, surprises had a terrible tendency to be bad.

She was trying to read his eyes as he hesitated

over his answer, so he turned away and headed for the door. He stopped in the doorway to add quickly, "Try to eat something at lunch. I'll give your doctor a call and see what you can do about keeping food down."

Then he walked away.

Chapter Five

He was going to be a father. Killian thought about that as he drove his white Jaguar back to the city. He'd ignored Daniel's insistence that *he* drive him back. He needed to be alone with the news. It had a curiously effervescent quality as it settled inside him and became a part of who he was.

A father! His own father, though a very busy man, had extended himself to be a part of Killian's and Sawyer's everyday lives when their mother had had so little to do with them. He'd told them stories about their grandfather, and how he sometimes hadn't seen him for months when he'd been trying to cultivate business overseas and ocean travel had been the most-used mode of transportation.

Killian considered the things he'd learned from his father. A deep sense of responsibility to his family, a strong work ethic, a sense of obligation to his employees that put them right in line of importance behind his family, a love of business that embraced its difficulties as well as the thrills involved in it and a determination to be smart but ethical in all his dealings.

His father had often told him that when he'd been young, he'd had a tendency to gamble and run with a crowd of privileged elites who intended to enjoy their wealth and answer to no one.

But the business had needed an influx of new capital, and he'd married Susannah. In sympathy to his mother, Killian wondered for a moment what it would be like to suspect that you'd been given in marriage as an economic move. She'd been so beautiful that knowing it still had come down to money had to have been demoralizing.

As Killian recalled, though, his father had made brilliant use of that capital and had therefore been able to give Susannah everything a woman could want. He tried hard to remember those nights when she'd waved from the nursery door in her gowns and jewels, and couldn't remember that she'd seemed unhappy—just…eager to be off. Even at five years of age he'd understood that she hadn't wanted to be slowed down by the childish stories waiting on the tip of his tongue to tell, by the hugs he yearned to give—and get.

He shook off those thoughts and concentrated on today—this moment. His weirdly powerful happiness at the prospect of fatherhood existed outside of his confusion about Cordie, the memories of Abby and his concerns about the November Corporation. For the first time in—God! In years!—except for that first month of his marriage to Cordie…he was exhilarated.

He glanced at the speedometer, saw that he was driving over eighty miles an hour and slowed down, telling himself to concentrate on the road. Then he smiled to himself. The notion of prospective fatherhood was powerful fuel.

AT THE ABBOTT BUILDING he stopped in at Lew Weston's office on his way to his own. It was half the size of his and cluttered with paper, reports on other businesses and newspapers from all over the world. On Lew's walls were charts that only he understood, except for the wall reserved for photos of his family. He had two boys and two girls, ranging in ages from three to ten, and a wife who'd once been a television star.

His life was every jock's dream, and Lew, five foot ten, thirty pounds overweight, business nerd and Jackie Chan–movies junkie, had it.

Lew was focused on a report on top of the rubble on his desk and Killian had to rap on the door to get his attention.

Lew looked up and grinned. "Hey, Highness! Did I really hear that you went *home* for lunch? With a certain leggy redhead who shall remain nameless because of your propensity for shooting steam through your ears when her name is mentioned?"

"Yes, you did," Killian confirmed. "You got a minute?"

"Sure, come on in." Lew gestured to a chair near

his desk, then saw that it was stacked with his research fallout.

Killian beckoned for him to follow. "Let's talk in my office, where there's actually room to sit down."

Lew got up to comply. "Not nice to abuse the underlings," he grumbled.

"You're not an underling," Killian said over his shoulder as they walked past Barbara's desk. She waved at them while talking on the telephone. "You know more about the details of this company than I do. Coffee?"

"Please. You have the best coffee in the building."

Killian tossed his briefcase and jacket at the leather sofa and went to the bar to hit the brew button. Barbara always prepared the pot for a fresh brew when he was gone.

He took his chair while Lew sat in the one that faced his desk. Then he buzzed Barbara.

"Yes?" she asked.

"Will you get me Dr. Rosenkrantz, please?" he asked.

"Are you feeling ill?" she asked in concern.

He had to smile. "No. She's an obstetrician on Tenth Street."

There was silence for a long moment, then she replied dutifully, "Right away."

Lew arched an eyebrow, his eyes alight with interest. "An obstetrician? Is Cordie…?"

"Yes." Killian ran a hand over his face, finally relaxing a little in Lew's company. Though he loved and trusted his brothers, he was the eldest, and long habit required that he always appear in charge. Killian and Lew had roomed together in college, and Lew knew all his fears and weaknesses.

"Are you…back together?" Lew asked carefully.

Killian made a helpless gesture with both hands. "I don't know. Yes. For the length of her pregnancy, anyway."

Lew stared at him. "Then what?"

Killian shrugged, resettling in his chair. "We go our separate ways, I guess."

Lew continued to stare, confusion now wrinkling his forehead—and Lew was never confused about anything. "I'm not getting this. Why is she staying with you now if you're not staying together afterward?"

"Because she's not eating well," Killian said, "and she's lugging boxes around and generally not taking very good care of herself."

"And you're worried about her," Lew guessed.

"I'm worried about the baby," Killian corrected.

"Well, they're kind of one and the same, aren't they? I mean, you can't separate the two until she delivers. And even then, mother and child are forever linked." Lew sat up sharply and an apologetic expression crossed his face. He knew about Killian's past and apparently thought he'd made a thoughtless remark. If Killian hated one thing about his mother's abandonment and his little sister's disappearance—apart from the fact that both events had ripped his heart out—it was that everyone second-guessed his reaction to any reference to mothers, sisters, family, kidnap and a hundred other loosely related subjects.

"Well, usually they are," Lew said quietly. "Your mother was a sort of bad mutation."

Killian acknowledged that with a grim laugh. "Creates a picture of her with gills and antennae."

Lew smiled, too. "I'm sorry."

"Not necessary." Killian glanced at his watch. "We've got about ten minutes before our appointment with McCann–McGinnis. You caught any rumblings about the November Corporation?"

Lew frowned. "They've hired Stanford Intelligence."

Killian leaned back in his chair. Stanford Intelligence was a collection of legal, business, financial and investigative professionals who gathered information for companies planning to acquire or take over businesses, or to defend themselves from such things. They collected details on key investors, corporate officers, directors and shareholders, potential legal and regulatory compliance issues. And often they gained access to personal information that could affect a key player's performance and therefore a company's bottom line.

So the November Corporation was collecting information in preparation for making a move on Abbott Mills. "I knew the day was coming."

"I wouldn't worry about it yet," Lew said. "The old man's just posturing. He might just look at our picture, decide we're much too healthy to try a takeover and back off."

Killian nodded, but thought that old man Girard could just as well decide that *healthy* was appealing and put the wheels in motion.

"Well, I might be distracted for a little while," Killian said, pushing his chair back to the bar to pour two cups of coffee. He stood and carried the cups to his desk to avoid a spill, then sat down again. "Keep an eye on the situation for me and tell me when I should worry." He drew himself to the desk.

"I'll do that. Is Cordie the distraction?"

"Yeah. She tends to blur my focus."

"That's all right. You're allowed to have feelings as well as brilliant business inspirations." He grinned winningly. "I'm here."

Killian sipped his coffee and studied his friend with interest. "You have four little children. Why aren't you distracted all the time?"

"Because Karen's smart and capable and I'm certain she's taking care of everything."

"But…why aren't you worried about Karen?"

"Because I'm taking care of her."

"But you're not there—you're here."

Lew didn't see a problem. "She knows I adore her, that she's my life, that I'd die for her in a minute and that I trust her completely to keep our lives together, and every spare moment I have is devoted to her and the kids. So she understands the sometimes long nights at the office, and the plans that can change on a moment's notice. I guess…trust gives you peace so you *can* focus."

Killian nodded. Trust. That was the hitch right there.

"Will you share custody of the baby?" Lew asked. There were few secrets between them. Lew knew the details of Killian's divorce, and Killian knew that Polly Weston was having trouble reading, Charlie, though only six, was clearly headed for a lifetime of crime, Julie ate nothing but peanut butter and Oreos and Danny refused to be potty-trained.

"The baby's an Abbott," Killian replied. "It should live at Shepherd's Knoll."

Lew narrowed his gaze. "You mean, without Cordie?"

"Frankly, I don't know what I mean," Killian replied with a sigh. He leaned back and put his feet up on his desk. He seldom got that relaxed in his working environment, but he was a mass of contradictions at the moment and unloading on someone was comforting. "I don't want to be left out of the baby's life. Still, there's too much mistrust and too many hard feelings between Cordie and me for us ever to live together permanently."

"You two were so happy in the beginning," Lew said quietly. "It was as though she'd remade you into a happy workaholic instead of just the kind but unsmiling workaholic you used to be. Then it all stopped."

Killian took a long sip of his coffee. "The reason for that was pretty clear," he finally said.

Lew shook his head. "It stopped before you found her in bed with Brian. That was just the catalyst.

Something was changing prior to that." Lew leaned his elbows on his knees. "You didn't like being happy, did you?"

Killian rolled his eyes impatiently, dropped his feet and sat up. "That's ridiculous. I liked being happy. I just didn't like being distracted all the time. All she wanted to do was play and party, and I have 4,026 employees depending on me to keep their paychecks rolling in."

"Actually 4,029," Lew corrected. "You forgot the new night watchmen at the Massachusetts mill."

"See? All I did was take her home and already I've forgotten three employees."

Lew laughed, then sobered again. "I think that if you want to father this baby, you have to find a way to get along with Cordie. And if you want the baby to live with you, Cordie's got to be part of the package."

"She's not wild about me, either."

"No wonder. You're an idiot. She loved you like a madwoman, and I'll wager she still does. I know you haven't wanted to talk about it, but Karen heard from her while she was in Scotland. Cordie was devastated that you didn't believe her about Brian."

"Lew, I opened the hotel-room door and found them together."

"Cordie told Karen he'd switched rooms with her because her room didn't lock."

"The hotel would have given her another room."

"It was 2:00 a.m. after a long day of meetings and a late dinner. Brian gave her his key and told her he'd get another room for himself. She didn't suspect, of course, that he had a second key. Then up you come, looking for her..."

"If no one told the desk she'd moved into his room, why did they send me to his when I asked for her room number, instead of sending me to the room that didn't lock?"

Lew shrugged. "That's the mystery. If Brian set this all up to cause a split between you two, he could have just slipped a hundred to the desk clerk and asked him to give you his room number instead of hers and to call him when you were coming up. It would have been an easy thing to let himself into the room when you were on the elevator. He probably slipped into the room just as you were arriving, leaving her very little time to react or—she claims she'd been asleep—even to know what was going on when she woke up and saw you in the doorway and Brian in her room."

Killian had never believed Cordie's story and therefore never speculated on how a plot could have been worked out. Still, he found Lew's scenario doubtful.

"That's too preposterous to be possible."

"My whole life is too preposterous to be possible, yet it is. Open up your mind, Killian. You do it for business. Try it with people."

"I can imagine Brian wanting to find a way to hurt me, even destroy me. His father was after mine for years. Brian can't stand being second best. But what satisfaction would he get from simply breaking us up? It's not as though there'd be any financial benefit to him. The prenup only allowed Cordie ten percent of Abbott Mills stock, and my brothers and my stepmother and I have sixty percent of it. Even when she left with her stock, we still had controlling shares. So it's not like it would help November Corporation in a takeover bid.''

Lew nodded. ''I don't understand his motivations, either. Just yours. You wanted her out of your life and fell for that stupid setup.''

''They were acquainted with each other before she knew me. They have a history.''

''One of your best qualities as a boss,'' Lew said, ''is that you let everyone speak his or her piece. You always listen to grievances, new ideas, complaints, everything. Your employees say you're the fairest man they know. I think so, too. Except where Cordie's concerned. You should take time to examine why that is. Maybe November thought your breaking up with her would destroy you and you'd make stupid decisions that might endanger the company and help their cause.''

The intercom buzzed.

Killian, long familiar with Lew's candor, ignored the jibe as he depressed the Answer button.

''Dr. Rosenkrantz on line one,'' Barbara said. ''Sorry for the delay. She was with a patient.''

''Thank you, Barbara.''

Before picking up the call, Killian sent Lew a wry look. ''I'll be coming to you for kid advice. I'll expect you to be more sympathetic.''

Lew stood and dramatically put a hand to his heart. "You can count on me. See you in the conference room in—" he glanced at his watch "—five minutes."

Killian waved to indicate that he'd be there as he picked up the phone. "Dr. Rosenkrantz, this is Killian Abbott, Cordelia Abbott's husband. I need some information and some advice."

CORDIE PUT all her things away, then tried to lure Versace out of the bathroom, and when he refused, she sat in the middle of her bed in the circular room and made a few phone calls. She called her parents to tell them where she was.

"It's working?" Her mother's words were half question, half exclamation.

"So-so," Cordie replied. "And…I have something to tell you."

"What?" her father asked warily. "I told you it was risky."

Risky. That was an understatement.

"No, this part's just good," she said, convinced it was. "You're going to be grandparents around the middle of October."

Her mother squealed. Her father gasped.

"Darling, that's wonderful!" her mother said after a moment. "I mean…we're thrilled, but are you all right? Your life is so uncertain at this point in time.…"

Another understatement.

"This baby is a certainty I like having in my

life,'' Cordie said firmly. ''Whatever comes, I'm having this baby and it's mine.''

''How does Killian feel?'' Her father was always the one to focus on reality.

''He brought me to stay with him because he was worried about the baby,'' she said, injecting a smile into her voice.

''Not worried about you?''

''We're pretty closely connected at the moment.''

There was a pause, then her father said heavily, ''It's the point when you're no longer closely connected that I worry about. As I recall from the wedding, those Abbotts are very big on family pride.''

''So are you, Dad.''

''Damn right. I'm going to have my lawyer ready, just in case Killian tries to pull a fast one and you need counsel.''

''Good idea.'' She was humoring him. As though young Farley Johnson, who was so allergic to everything that grew on the eastern seaboard that he couldn't speak a sentence without sneezing from April to September, would be any competition for any of the lawyers Killian employed.

''Anyway, I just wanted you to know where I am. You can still reach me on my cell phone, or you probably still have the phone numbers from before. And you can always get me at the store.''

''So you're still working.''

''Absolutely.''

''You call us if you need us,'' her father ordered.

''I will, but don't worry. I feel fine, and Kezia

will take very good care of me.'' She didn't mention that the cook had fixed Cordie an omelette that had been delicious for the first few bites but then had refused to go down. A handful of crackers, however, nibbled on slowly, were appeasing her hunger.

"White rice worked for me," her mother said.

"I'll try that."

They ended their conversation with the promise that she would keep in touch every few days, or they would call if they didn't hear from her.

That chore successfully completed, she stabbed out the number of Abbott's West to see how they were managing without her.

"We're doing fine," Candy reassured her, "except that Eleanor thinks she's the boss when you're not here and is trying to tell everyone what to do. Hunter's taking notes."

Oh, dear. "She *is* assistant manager," Cordie reminded her, "but I'll be there tomorrow, so there's nothing for everyone to get upset about."

"Except that she's got us unpacking purses that arrived this morning because accessories is down a clerk today. We have these straw hobo bags that are making me sneeze, and Hunter won't work on unpacking freight because she says she was hired for women's wear and that doesn't include accessories. So I'm doing everything myself. If I sneeze once more, I'll dislocate something."

Cordie pleaded Candy's case with Eleanor. "And I'll be there tomorrow to help out."

"You let these kids run all over you," Eleanor

complained. "And you do the hard stuff so you don't have to listen to them complain. Well, Mr. Abbott told me to make sure you don't do any more heavy lifting and that we all pitch in with the grunt work. I'm just doing what I'm told." She lowered her voice. "And if that little dissident Hunter doesn't stop taking notes on me, I'm going to ship her out with the returns!"

Cordie counted to ten. She didn't let the young employees run all over her, but she did try to put them to work on the projects they enjoyed. It made for a happier ship. And she didn't mind helping with everything, because it kept her in touch with the details of the department.

As for Hunter, she was a good employee when she felt she was being treated fairly, though Cordie recognized that she did pose a problem it was wise to be careful about.

"Did belts and shoes come in, too?"

"Yes, but we always do purses first because they're bigger and take more—"

"I know," Cordie interrupted. "Candy can start on those. There's less likely to be anything in the leather to aggravate her allergies. And let Hunter wait on customers while you work on purses. Having to stop stocking and go back to the register anyway is always annoying."

Eleanor gasped. "When you're gone, I'm management. I'm checking invoices and preparing tags. I don't have to carry goods around."

This time Cordie counted to twenty. "I thought

you said Mr. Abbott asked you all to pitch in with the grunt work?''

There was a moment's pout. ''But when you're gone, I'm—''

''Management, I know. But every good manager pitches in to help.''

''Not when you're working with a whiner and a Nazi.''

''Eleanor...''

''All right. But I'm not happy. Maybe I'll have to start making notes of my own. Is there anything else?''

Cordie had to force a congenial tone. ''No. Just that I'll be back tomorrow. I'll come in early. With doughnuts.''

''All right,'' Eleanor relented. ''See you then.''

Cordie hung up the phone and lay back against the pillows. It was late afternoon, and even considering the bizarre quality of the day, she decided things could be going in a much worse direction than they were so far.

Killian could have been furious about the baby instead of just concerned and interfering. As hungry as she was, if it was easy for her to eat, she'd probably have fifty pounds to lose when the baby was born, and the hostile reception she'd expected from Killian's family and staff hadn't materialized. So all in all, the plot was holding its own.

True, she hadn't anticipated that he might want to *keep* the baby without taking her back, but she had five months in which to change his mind about that. She had to get smart and creative.

If only she knew how.

She heard a growl and looked over the side of the bed to see Versace peering around the corner of the bathroom door. He took several cautious steps, still growling. She often thought of him as having a siren attached. When he was frightened, he ran through her apartment, meowing loudly in a sort of kitty version of "The sky is falling! The sky is falling!" When he was trying to intimidate, he lowered the pitch on his siren and growled as he moved—this, the feline version of "Me? Are you talkin' to me?"

"Hi, Sachi!" she exclaimed, delighted to finally see him out of the bathroom. He started at the sound of her voice and turned to arch his back at her. Then he seemed to recognize her and he leaped onto the bed.

On the coverlet, he jumped two feet into the air when he came nose to snap-tab with her Daytimer. She stroked him from ears to tail and told him over and over that everything would be all right.

As she stretched out on the bed again, suddenly tired, he climbed onto her stomach and leaned forward to sniff cautiously at the pillow behind her. His considerable weight on the small points of his four feet was painful and she pushed gently on him until he lay down.

He finally settled on her rib cage, his paws on her breasts, and began to purr. His siren was a truly adaptable tool.

"Everything will be fine," she told him, scratching between his ears. "We'll be just fine." She had herself convinced as she dozed off.

Half an hour later, Killian appeared in her bedroom doorway and Versace deepened her navel about an inch in his haste to escape into the bathroom.

Chapter Six

"That's one fraidy cat," Killian said, taking a few steps into the room. "Are you okay?"

She sat up, unconsciously putting a hand up to her hair. She was sure she looked scary. "I'm fine." She patted the too-tight jeans she'd pulled on in an attempt to protect herself from the cat's claws. "What are you doing home so early?"

He held up a white thermal bag with a dated but familiar logo on it. A man in a soda-jerk hat, white shirt and bow tie leaned out to wave from a truck that bore the name Hudson River Ice Cream.

Her mouth began to water. Next to Killian and his family, the ice-cream shop in town was what she'd liked best about Losthampton. She salivated at the thought of her favorite flavor.

"You didn't!" she said in a reverent whisper, her eyes glued to the bag as he brought it closer.

"I did." He pulled out a half-gallon container, then instead of giving it to her detoured to the bathroom.

She got up to follow him and collided with him

as he walked out again with a clean hand towel wrapped around the carton. She took it from him and held it to her, unaware of the cold.

"Is it...?" she asked, desperate for a spoon.

He reached into the bag he'd left on the bed and handed her a sturdy, flat wooden spoon that accompanied all Hudson River Ice Cream. Then he removed the lid, creamy vanilla ice cream and orange-sherbet swirl adhering to the inside of the top as he pulled it off. Handling the lid carefully, he placed it upside down on a small desk in a corner.

"Barber-pole ice cream," Cordie said in disbelief, staring at it as though she'd been handed a carton of diamonds. Other producers of ice cream had a combination of vanilla and orange sherbet, but none of them was the perfect, creamy texture Hudson River's was.

She dipped the spoon in to the carton, put the ice cream in her mouth to dissolve and felt the three months she'd been married to Killian come back in the sensory memory of barber-pole ice cream. He'd laughed at her, saying she was the only person he knew who'd walk through a snowdrift for ice cream.

She hadn't cared. Kezia kept a supply in the kitchen freezer, and Cordie and Killian had made the ice-cream shop one of their regular stops on weekends, whatever the weather.

The ice cream went down, cool and comforting. She waited for the nausea that assaulted her almost immediately now when she ate anything. But nothing happened.

Killian, waiting with her, raised an eyebrow.

She took another tentative bite. This one was even more delicious than the first. She sank onto the edge of the bed with a groan.

Killian sat beside her worriedly. "Making you sick?" he asked, reaching for the carton.

She held it protectively to her with two hands. "No! No, it's wonderful." She put another spoonful in her mouth. "Oh, wow."

"Okay, but you can't eat the whole carton. Dr. Rosenkrantz said to eat whatever you thought would go down and stay down until you get over the nausea. Whatever will sustain you is good enough for now. Later, we'll worry about getting the right nutrition."

Intoxicated by the luxury of eating something that didn't fight back and that was also one of her favorite things in the whole world, she said sincerely, "You're a genius, Killian."

"YEAH." He resisted the urgent need to touch her. She looked even paler than she had this morning, but her wide eyes had brightened when she'd seen the ice-cream carton. He'd suspected some time had elapsed since she'd eaten anything that tasted good, but she'd taken the nausea all pretty lightly and he hadn't realized just how desperate she was until he'd seen her face transformed by the taste of the ice cream. Now he feared surgery would be required to get the carton back from her.

She was still spooning.

"Can you save some until dinner?" he asked, amused but also concerned.

"No," she said simply.

He put a hand to her back to make contact with her. He was afraid she'd forgotten he was here. Her eyes focused on the ice cream, she answered him as though he were just some disembodied voice, trying to interfere with her pleasure.

"Cordie," he said, preparing to argue for possession of the spoon.

But he didn't have to. She stopped the instant he touched her, the ice-cream spell broken. She looked into his eyes, and for an instant, put him under *her* spell.

Inexplicably, he saw what was in her mind—that happy first month of their marriage. The bliss of souls connecting, hearts touching, bodies entwined in the happiness of discovery. Long weekend walks in the snow, Trivial Pursuit on the floor in front of the fireplace, Sunday mornings at the bakery with the newspaper spread out on the table between them.

Then, without warning, Brian Girard's face superimposed itself on his memories. But for the first time since the Brian debacle, he felt the smallest uncertainty over what might have happened.

Startled by that turn of events, he, too, came out of his spell. He noticed that the carton had gone slack in her hands. Acting quickly, he took it from her.

Her lips parted in surprise, and unable to stop himself, he pushed aside the old anger and resentment that suddenly didn't seem to know where it belonged and leaned down to kiss her lips. She tasted of orange and vanilla and that curious sweetness he'd never been able to identify but attributed to her femininity.

Turbulence moved in him as the anger and resentment tried to reassert itself. But her pale face reflected such surprise and delight, he simply couldn't trust those old emotions.

While she was still distracted, he snatched the spoon and stuck it in the top of the ice cream. "Dinner's in an hour," he said. "Why don't you rest, and I'll have Kezia serve you a bowl of ice cream."

She blinked, apparently as confused as he felt. Then she nodded and smiled. "Okay," she said quietly. "That would be nice."

He never did get to the dinner table. Lew called with an alternative plan for the copy in one of the ads they'd discussed that afternoon. They'd liked the basic idea, but thought the copy lacked punch.

Lew faxed the ideas, then called so they could discuss them. Killian could hear Lew's children in the background, laughing and shouting at one another. He felt a small stab of envy, then a little ripple of excitement. That could be him one day, working from home, where his children played around him.

He quickly dismissed the idea, realizing he was getting the cart way before the horse. The woman he no longer intended to be married to was pregnant with one child who might not even live with him— at least not all the time. Despite his posturing, he knew he couldn't fight Cordie for full custody. She was in love with this baby already.

Focusing on the ad, he listened to Lew's ideas, contributed a few of his own and finally agreed on one of the concepts. When he checked the clock, it was after 9:00 p.m.

He went down to the kitchen, to find that Kezia had left him a plate of pork roast, vegetables and red potatoes in the refrigerator. He microwaved the food and took it back to the small table in the library, where he had time to catch up on a few memos from various departments. Daniel and Kezia had gone home and his brothers were off to a bachelor party in Southhampton.

He was distracted from his work, though, by the silence of the house. He was so seldom at home during the week these days, that he'd forgotten how quiet it was. He was reminded of his childhood. He'd been a terrible insomniac in those days, and had wandered around the big house at night while his mother was out at some function and his father was locked in his study. Killian had been quite comfortable with the creaks and sighs of the place, but he used to sit in the big chair in the parlor and imagine the house filled with people who didn't work all the time or go out all the time.

He remembered clearly thinking that when he was an adult, he would have parties at least once a week, with music and dancing and continuous laughter.

He looked around him at the quiet and felt a real regret for that lost dream. Circumstances had conspired against him, filling his life with a sadness difficult to push away. He'd managed somewhat by focusing his energies on the business, but escaping a personal life forever was impossible.

And now he was faced with a personal life bigtime. He was going to be a father.

That little thrill rippled through him again. He stood still in surprise at how reliable that was. Even the smallest thought about the baby…there it was again…a little flap of excitement, a sensation of something new deep inside his carefully tended reserve. Hope. Promise.

He was at the bar for a cup of coffee when he noticed a shadow move in the darkness past the French doors. Security always on his mind, he was momentarily on guard, but he saw that the figure wasn't moving at all furtively.

The security lights at the front and the back of the house didn't reach to the garden. Winfield had insisted on installing one there, but his brothers had complained that the brightness kept them awake at night, so he'd removed the light. They'd planted a thistle hedge, instead, to discourage intruders.

He went to the French doors and yanked them open, illumination from the library spilling out onto the porch and garden—casting a golden glow on Cordie, in a silky robe, sniffing a bush of orange honeysuckle.

She gaped in surprise, her fingers still cupped around a handful of blossoms. His breath caught in his throat. She'd brushed her hair out, obviously in preparation for bed, and the light from the library cast ripples in it. She resembled a figure in a Pre-Raphaelite painting.

He had to clear his throat to speak. "What are you doing?" he asked, going down the steps.

She took one last whiff of the flowers, then came to join him. "I was getting ready for bed and opened my window and caught the fragrance of honeysuckle. I really miss flowers in the city. Got your work finished?"

"Yes." He helped her up the steps and gestured her into the library. She went past him and he saw that the robe was a pale green that flattered her redhead's complexion—and that the whole romantic image was destroyed by the wildly colored woolen booty-slippers on her feet. "Were you able to eat any dinner?"

She stopped in the middle of the room and looked around herself, smiling gently with apparently pleasant memories. He suddenly remembered that they'd made love in this room in front of the fire one cold January afternoon.

Her eyes went to the fireplace, then to his and lingered there for a moment, that fragile little smile still in place. Then she turned away from him abruptly and pointed to his half-finished dinner and the work spread around it on the table.

"I had more ice cream. I see you didn't do very well with dinner, either."

"I'm still working on it," he said.

"Speaking of work…" She folded her arms, assuming a somewhat aggressive stance in the silly slippers. "I'm going in tomorrow with you and Daniel."

He knew this would come up. "Yes," he agreed.

She stared at him in momentary surprise, then nodded. "Good, then. I was afraid you didn't trust me to stay out of the stock."

"I don't," he replied. "That's why you're coming to work in the Abbott Building, not at the store."

Another stare. "There's no women's wear in the Abbott Building." She seemed to rethink that. "Well, yes, the women there are wearing things, but you know what I mean."

"I do," he said. "You've been temporarily reassigned to me to wrap up plans for the annual meeting."

She closed her eyes and expelled an impatient breath. When she opened them again, they snapped at him. "I'm the buyer for Abbott Mills Women's Wear Department, not some coffee-pouring, telephone-answering flunky to the boss whose job was created to keep her from wrestling boxes he thinks are too heavy for her. I said I'd be more careful—"

He cut her off with a smile. "I know you did, but I don't believe you. You'll get all involved and forget that you're not supposed to be carrying freight around. Or your team members will argue with one another and you'll do the job yourself to save time. Dr. Rosenkrantz thinks the reassignment is a good idea." That was only partially true, but the subterfuge could lend weight to his argument.

Cordie studied him dubiously. "She told me I was perfectly healthy and, except for the nausea problem, could do pretty much what I wanted. And she shouldn't be talking to you about me, anyway."

He nodded, deciding to go with the half truths. "We dealt only in hypotheticals. I asked for general pregnancy advice, and she tried to help me. Upshot is she told me that it's important to keep your strength up with walks and good food, but if you're not eating well, to soft-pedal the exercise until you are."

"My department's in a mess!" she complained with sudden urgency. "The staff are great when I'm there, but leave them alone and they start bickering like little kids. I promised I'd be back tomorrow to—"

"I'll send someone to replace you until after the annual meeting. Dr. Rosenkrantz says your nausea problem could be corrected quickly. You should be eating better by the meeting."

She narrowed her eyes at him. "You seem to be on cozy terms with the doc for someone who didn't know she existed until this morning. Or are you making all this up to get your own way?"

"I don't have to make things up to get my way," he replied, trying not to smile. "I'm the boss."

She ignored that. "I don't believe you talked to her," she challenged.

He was going to enjoy this part. "The last time she saw you was the twenty-third of May, when she asked you to call her if you continued to have trouble with nausea. She prescribed a vitamin and told you she wanted you to build yourself up.'' She didn't have to know that information had come from Trilby.

She looked taken aback, her suspicions dissolving.

She angled her chin. ''Some general confirmation. You realize this will put us in proximity all the time,'' she said on a warning note. ''Not only will I be underfoot here at home but at the office, as well. Will you be able to deal with that? I mean, considering you're convinced I fooled around on you with another man and generally made your life a misery?''

''I'll do my best to handle it,'' he countered. ''And I never said you made my life a misery.''

''It was implied.''

''Yeah, well, let's talk facts, not implications. All I said was that we turned out to be wrong for each other.''

She sighed and met his gaze. ''That's where the real heartbreak is in this,'' she said quietly. ''Because that isn't entirely true. I may have turned out to be wrong for you, but you were *everything* for me.'' She caught her breath as though that had been painful to say. ''Good night.''

She made a chin-up exit, the silky robe swirling around her ankles in the loud and woolly slippers. That outfit was a metaphor for who she was, a woman who could be loud and prickly one minute and smooth as silk against your face the next.

God. Dealing with her made his childhood look like a walk in the park.

CORDIE STUDIED herself in the ladies'-room mirror on the twenty-third floor of the Abbott Building and burst into tears. This was her fourth day working in a spacious office down the hall from Killian's and she hated it!

Well, she didn't *hate* it hate it, but the work was so much less interesting than buying and selling clothes. Well, working on preparations for the annual meeting wasn't *un*interesting, but it wasn't as exciting as knowing she could turn every woman who walked into the store into a goddess or a sprite, depending on whether she wanted something formal or casual.

In a blue or gray suit, with a short haircut, every woman around here looked like a man. Her brightly colored dresses and suits stuck out like a gaudy paper flower in a garden of ferns. A gaudy paper flower whose leaves no longer fit!

She retied the waistband of her pale blue slacks with a safety pin and dropped the popped button into her pocket. Fortunately, the colorful tunic shirt she had on over the pants would hide the fashion faux pas. But what would she do about her face? Her already freckled complexion was suddenly blotchy and suggested she was in the last stages of some killer rosacea.

Her hair was the only part of her thriving in this pregnancy, but in this fern-garden environment, she was careful to keep it in a long braid or wound in a knot at the back of her head.

How was she ever going to lure Killian back to

her looking like this? Or feeling like this? She hated everything today.

She'd been happy with what she'd accomplished the past several days: she'd found a caterer on Long Island who could help Kezia with the food, a rental company to provide tables and chairs and a pavilion for meetings outside; and she'd gotten Trilby to locate several secretaries willing to help at staff meetings and act as gofers.

But the first thing this morning, the rental company had called to tell her the large pavilion she wanted would be in use at another party that day and wondered if she'd settle for two smaller ones. And the caterer had misread his calendar and wouldn't be available for that weekend after all.

She'd tried to call Trilby for sympathy and advice, but Trilby was at home, sick.

She'd headed back to her desk, thinking she needed coffee. Of course, she shouldn't have coffee, so she settled for tea, which just wasn't bringing her to the sharp edge of her wits.

She went back to her office and sat down behind her desk to look through the phone book for another caterer. The first two she contacted needed more notice than a week's time. She was about to contact a third, when there was a rap on her door and Killian's head and shoulders appeared around it.

"Hi," he said. "How about if you and I and Lew go to lunch at one and you can tell us how plans for the meeting are progressing?"

She burst into tears, astonishing herself and causing Killian to take off and close the door behind him.

At least, that was what she thought had happened as she heard the door close. Fishing for a tissue in her side drawer, her eyes blurred with sudden and unexpected tears, she presumed he simply didn't have time for hysteria.

So when he walked around her desk, sat on the edge of it and leaned toward her with a hand on her shoulder, she looked up at him in shock.

"What's the matter?" he asked in concern. And he really did seem worried—about the baby, of course, not about her.

She tried to answer and couldn't. She finally had him within touching distance and she looked as though she'd been power-washed before repainting. And she was blubbering, to boot.

"Do you feel sick?" he asked gently, leaning down into her averted face. "I'll ask Daniel to take you home."

She shook her head fiercely. "I'm not sick," she said in a pathetic squeak. "I'm just…suicidal!"

"Oh, well. That's not a problem." He caught her chin in his hand and grinned at her. "None of the windows open."

She wanted to frown at him for being smart, but he was behaving so much like the Killian from that first month of their marriage that she wanted to throw her arms around him, instead.

Haltingly, she poured out the whole sad story of her morning—the caterer and the rental company, the waistband of her pants, her complexion and her virulent hatred today of everything in her life. She didn't mention the garden of ferns.

He took both her hands, pulled her out of her chair, walked her to the small flowered sofa against the wall and sat beside her.

He was going to tell her she was fired, she thought, that her instability was causing a prob—

Her thought processes stopped abruptly when he put an arm around her and drew her close. "Relax, Cordie," he said softly. "It'll all come together."

Afraid to focus on his comforting touch, she tried, instead, to explain her desperation. "But the meeting's just a week away, and everything I thought was done is now *un*done and—"

"If we can't find a pavilion, we'll just keep everyone inside for the meeting and let them wander the grounds on their free time. And if we can't find a caterer, we'll get stuff from the deli or somewhere. It's certainly nothing to cry about."

"I popped my button," she explained feebly, finally allowing herself to lean into him. He pulled her near and wrapped a hand around her upper arm to hold her there. She wallowed in the strength of his grip.

"Popped your button," he said. "Is that anything like flipping your lid?"

She ignored the attempt at humor. She didn't want to be amused out of this delicious moment. "It means the waist of my pants doesn't fit anymore."

"But that's supposed to happen." His voice was

a quiet, comforting rumble. "The baby can't grow if you don't."

"I feel ugly," she argued.

"You're not ugly," he countered gallantly.

"Oh, yeah?" She leaned her head back against his arm so he could see her face. "I look as though I have some rare skin disease."

"It's just an increased secretion of oils caused by hormonal changes," he said, going over her feature by feature with a curious indulgence in his eyes that she hadn't seen there since they were first married. "Just like your mercurial moods. It's just hormones. A normal, natural part of the whole process."

"How do you know about hormonal changes and mood swings?" she asked in surprise.

"Lew explained it all to me," he confessed without embarrassment. "He has four little kids, remember. He's been through this four times. It's also in the book."

"What book?"

"I forget the title. Something about staying sane if your wife's pregnant. Lew lent it to me."

She loved that he kept referring to her as his wife without putting *ex* or *former* in front of it. Then he opened her clenched right fist, took the tissue she'd been reaching for when he walked into the office and dabbed at her eyes. She was grateful she was sitting down or she'd have fallen down.

"So, what do you say? Lunch with me and Lew? We'll go somewhere where they have ice cream, so you don't have to just watch us eat."

She was winning him over, she thought in amazement. Or the baby was winning him over. That was probably closer to the truth. But as long as the baby was still contained within her, she reaped the benefits. She could live with that for now.

''The only thing I can tell you,'' she said frankly, sitting up and trying to pull herself together, ''is that all my plans have fallen apart.'' She regretted the movement instantly because it put her out of touch with his hand. To her relief, he simply moved it to a spot between her shoulder blades, where he rubbed gently. She had to bite her bottom lip to avoid moaning.

''We'll brainstorm together. Then we'll send Lew back to work and go buy you some new pants.''

She decided she could die right now, a happy woman. But with his warm hand on her back and that sweet expression in his eyes, she committed herself anew to her plot to restore her marriage in preparation for the arrival of their baby. She could do this.

She sniffed one last time and nodded. ''Okay,'' she said.

He kissed her temple and went to get his jacket.

She had to stop herself from reaching for him, pinning him to the sofa and initiating the deep kiss she really wanted.

Chapter Seven

Killian sat on a brocade-upholstered bench, his jacket and tie discarded, and watched Cordie study her reflection in a tall mirror. She'd just tried on several pairs of pants appropriate to work, but now sported jeans to replace the ones that choked her.

He'd been sure shopping would perk up her mood—even the mood controlled by rioting hormones. Shopping was a vast emotional experience for her, even beyond the simple delight it was for most women. Clothes were Cordie's career and she drew pleasure from the clever cut of a beautiful fabric, an inspired design; he'd even known her to get excited over just the right buckle or button. The herringbone trim soutache had once sent her into ecstasy.

She'd been close to her old self by the time they had lunch at a small grill down the block, where he and Lew often escaped to talk over problems they didn't want overheard at the office. Under Lew's sympathetic influence, she even made light of her emotional episode and insisted she'd have the whole project under control by tomorrow.

Killian was sure she would. She was always efficient in a work situation, or whenever she had to be.

But usually she just liked to enjoy the moment and go with whatever it brought her. As she was doing now.

Since shopping was major business for her, she'd unfastened the knot at the back of her head and her mass of red hair now swung saucily in a long ponytail. Her cheeks were pink, her eyes bright, and her smile was on full display.

She turned from the mirror to face him. "Do you like the jeans?" she asked, flashing up her blouse to expose the square elastic panel over her stomach.

He laughed. "I do. But that's now four pairs of pants. What about a dress for the dinner party the last night of the meeting?"

She glanced up at the clock. It was almost 3:00 p.m. "Do you have time to wait while I find something?" Then she suggested with a definite lack of enthusiasm, "Or you could return to work and I'll return on my own. It's only three blocks."

"I'll wait," he said.

"I think you have an appointment this afternoon."

He nodded. "I canceled it."

Her smile hiked up a notch as she and an eager clerk went to a rack of dresses.

He didn't know what he was doing. He'd called

Barbara while Cordie was putting on the first pair of pants to ask her to cancel his three o'clock appointment.

She was accustomed to moving appointments around. "Of course," she'd said. "Who are you meeting, instead?"

"I'm...shopping," he'd replied.

A moment's silence had followed on the other end of the line. "Shopping," she'd finally repeated.

"Yes. Cordie needs a few things."

"Ah." She said the small word with a sort of drawn-out satisfaction he tried to ignore.

"Not sure when I'll be back."

"Nothing earth-shattering going on at the moment," she replied. "Don't hurry."

"Thank you, Barbara." He'd hung up, realizing that he hadn't canceled an appointment for personal reasons since he'd taken over from his father.

Maybe he didn't have to know what he was doing, he speculated as Cordie and the clerk pulled several garments off the rack, talked them over, put one back, took another one. This was new territory. He was going to be a father.

Of course, Cordie wasn't new. In fact, Cordie in this mood, bright, excited, enjoying her life on a cellular level, was the Cordie he'd fallen in love with—all sparkle and charm and spellbinding vivacity.

Then he remembered this was the very Cordie he'd finally become afraid of.

Afraid of?

He was a little surprised to think in terms of fear. His father had taught him that nothing and no one could hurt him if he was honest and believed in himself. Then his mother had broken his heart when she'd left, and his little sister's disappearance had cut him wide-open.

But hurt and fear were not the same things. Though everyone had fear of being hurt, so the two were too closely allied to consider separately.

Okay, now he was confusing himself. But he had five months to make sense of it. All he knew was that they were enjoying each other's company, this was a time when she needed his support, and he felt a responding need to shelter her, care for her. And this concern for her seemed to exist apart from the Brian debacle. He still didn't understand what had happened, and right now at least, didn't have to.

He simply accepted the weird state of affairs.

He watched Cordie disappear into the dressing room, then return a few minutes later in a surprisingly snug black dress that clung everywhere and accentuated the still-small pooch of her tummy.

She came toward him, long legs moving gracefully, her ponytail sashaying from side to side. She put a long-fingered hand to her belly. "Do you think the dress is too daring?" she asked. "I mean, this is the way fashion's gone with pregnancy. We don't hide it anymore—we flaunt it. But would you be more comfortable, since it's a work thing, if I wore something more concealing?"

He had to consider that a minute. He'd always

claimed the annual meeting was a place where all attending could be genuine in a comfortable environment, share what was on their minds and give and take without fear of being evaluated on their candor.

"You look beautiful in it," he admitted. "And I can't imagine that pregnancy would offend anybody."

She seemed surprised. "So that's a yes?"

"That's an underlined yes."

She leaned down spontaneously to kiss him. He lifted his mouth to her, and what was supposed to have been a perfunctory thank-you lasted a little longer, went a little deeper.

He felt the cautious tip of her tongue, responded with his. Then he was on his feet, had her face in his hands and her arms looped around his neck.

He wrapped his arms around her as they reacted like lovers starved for each other's touch. Power surged through him as she melted against him, and he had a vivid memory of their wedding night. Their lovemaking had been a combination of emotional dynamite and sensual fireworks. He'd felt as though his life had started over, as though the past had never happened and the future had all sorts of opportunities he'd thought the past had made impossible—life without blame and guilt.

She pushed on his shoulders suddenly, wedging a space between them. She looked as surprised as he did and a little frightened. He didn't understand this at all, given her insistence in the beginning that she'd wanted him back.

He came down to earth, though not entirely. He wanted more, felt as though he *needed* more. He was somewhere in Middle Earth, like the Hobbits.

He dropped his hands from her and smiled, disliking the notion that he somehow frightened her. "Get the dress," he said, as though the earth hadn't moved between them and left a large pile of slag. "I like it."

"Okay," she whispered, and hurried off.

A stunned clerk smiled tentatively at him, then followed her.

They wandered back into the office shortly after four o'clock, he carrying her packages. Everyone stopped to look. She wore a bright pink dress the clerk had taken into the dressing room while Cordie was changing out of the black one. It was dotted with large, colorful flowers, and a drawstring at the empire waist could be loosened as her pregnancy progressed. She'd bought pink shoes with a slight wedge heel, and had tied her hair back up into a loose knot, tendrils spilling around her face.

She looked lush and happy, like some personification of Mother Earth. And he was strangely proud to be following behind her with everyone knowing that the little mound of her stomach exaggerated by the drawstring was his doing.

COMPLETELY REFRESHED by three scoops of coffee ice cream and a few hours of shopping—she refused to assess what the kiss had done to her—Cordie had another caterer on deck by the time they left for home.

Killian didn't mention the kiss, though he didn't seem at all uncomfortable that it had happened. So she decided to take her cue from his behavior.

For the next few days they rode to and from work together as they had been doing, met several times a day in his office to discuss various aspects of the annual meeting and generally behaved like two very good friends who could be married.

Though the whole situation made Cordie long for more touching, more kissing, more intimacy, her fear grew in proportion to their ease in being together. She was now more committed than ever to her little plot, but she was very much aware of what she stood to lose if this camaraderie was just a temporary thing.

What if he'd simply decided it was easier to be friends than antagonists while she was carrying their baby? What if his concern was just civility and not affection? What if, when she finally delivered, he fought for custody of the baby? Not only did she not want to relinquish her baby, but now that she saw Killian again as he used to be, she had no real desire to take their baby away from *him*.

So where did that leave her?

She decided not to think about it. She just had to believe that she had the ability to make this work out for both of them—all three of them.

When the phone rang late one evening after Daniel and Kezia had gone home, Cordie picked it up. Killian was working in the library, Sawyer had gone into town for dinner and Campbell had taken off with friends.

"Hello," she said. "Shepherd's Knoll."

"Hello," a genteel female voice replied cautiously. Cordie recognized it instantly as Chloe's. But apparently Chloe wasn't sure who she was. "Who is this?"

"Chloe!" Cordie exclaimed, excited to hear her. Then, remembering that Chloe might feel the animosity Cordie had expected from the rest of the household but been spared, she added more quietly, "It's me. Cordie."

"Cordie!" Chloe said with a rich guttural R. She did sound pleased. "Are you back?"

"Well…temporarily."

"Comment?" Chloe demanded in French.

"I'm back until the baby's born," Cordie replied, rolling her eyes at her poor choice of words. Such an announcement called for a little preparation.

Fortunately, Chloe hadn't quite grasped her meaning.

"What baby?" she asked.

"Our baby." Cordie drew a breath. "Killian and I are expecting a baby."

Chloe said several things in rapid, excited French that Cordie guessed suggested a happy response. "Why did he not tell me?"

"Well…he just found out—just after you left for Paris, I think." She explained about getting the job at Abbott Mills and the results of her physical exam that had startled the human resources director, who had called Killian. "How is Tante Bijou?"

"She's getting along," Chloe replied, "but she is enjoying having me here and I am reluctant to leave her. Although now that I'm about to become a grandmother…!"

"You have five months," Cordie put in quickly. "You can stay in Paris and speed her recovery."

"How are you feeling?"

"I'm well," Cordie replied. "A lot of morning sickness, but the doctor says I'm very healthy."

Chloe exclaimed in French again. "I cannot tell you how happy this news makes me. But I'd be happier if we stop talking about things being *temporary*. Let me speak to Killian."

The kitchen phone was a call director because Kezia often answered for the whole household when Winfield was busy. Cordie put Chloe on hold, pressed the number for the library and waited for Killian to pick up.

"Yes?" he asked.

"Your mom," she said, then hung up. Trying to explain to him that she'd told Chloe about the baby was just too complicated while Chloe waited on a transatlantic call.

Cordie spooned up a small dish of ice cream—the reason she'd come downstairs in the first place—and sat at a small table in a corner of the kitchen to eat. So far, ice cream was still the only food that would stay down without reprisal, and she still loved it, but she found herself longing for the taste of chicken, baked potato, any vegetable.

Killian appeared a few minutes later, stretching his arms and dropping his head to one shoulder, then the other, to relieve the tension.

"Thanks," he said with a dry smile in her direction as he went to the refrigerator for the carton of ice cream. "I'm in big trouble for not having called her the instant I knew you were pregnant." He held the carton up and asked over his shoulder, "You are sharing this?"

"Of course. I think it's community property."

"I bought it."

"Doesn't matter. And anyway, you bought it for me."

He spooned some into a bowl, returned the carton to the freezer, then came to sit opposite her at the table. "I have a few other things that are yours, which I've been keeping in the library safe."

She guessed instantly what they were. She felt a little burst of hope, but struggled to maintain a casual voice. "My ring," she said. "And my combs."

He nodded. "The combs would look great with that new black dress."

"They would," she agreed. But she was more interested in the ring.

"You want them back?" he asked. He was being as determinedly casual as she was.

"The combs?"

"Yes."

The little burst of hope went dark like spent

fireworks. She did want them. Though they weren't her wedding ring, they were something else he'd given her and she loved them, but she'd returned them in disappointment over his unwillingness to believe her about Brian, and nothing about that had changed.

Had he offered her the ring, she might have reacted differently, but he hadn't. And that contributed to a rising sense of annoyance.

"No, thank you," she said politely, though her tone could have floated an iceberg.

He seemed surprised. "I thought your purpose in getting a job with Abbott Mills was to get me back."

That revved her annoyance. "It was, then you made it clear that wasn't going to happen and I changed my mind."

His blue gaze met her dark eyes unflinchingly. "That must be why you kissed me as though you were starved for me that afternoon in the maternity shop."

"You kissed me," she corrected.

"You got into it."

"Yes. You'd been nice to me about the whole…hormone thing."

"So you were just being grateful."

Suddenly impatient with the conversation, she scraped her chair back and got to her feet. "What difference does it make what I was feeling? Nothing we do means anything since we're never going to reconnect in the old way because you're still mad at me for sleeping with Brian, which I didn't do, but you won't believe me…that would require your having faith in me and you don't have any faith left!''

She turned to stomp out of the kitchen, but he caught her arm and yanked her back. His eyes were stormy, his grip biting. She expected angry words and accusations. Instead, he demanded in a growl, ''What if I said I changed my mind about that?''

She stared at him for a full ten seconds. After all he'd put her through? Sending her away. The torturous weeks in Scotland. The desperation that had brought her back to end up here in his house, emotionally still miles from him.

''I'd say you're lying,'' she finally replied, trying to yank her arm away from him.

He held on. ''Oh, I'm supposed to believe your outrageous stories, but you don't have to believe me?''

''I had no ulterior motive!'' she shouted at him. ''The truth was all I had! *You* just want your baby and you're willing to do anything to keep me long enough for you to get it! Then it's adios Cordelia!''

''What? You're a mind reader now?''

''You *told* me that was your plan!''

''I *lied,* all right?'' he roared back at her, his always-in-control demeanor shattered. ''I *adored* you! Gave you everything it was in my power to give you, and I decided to surprise you at your hotel and found you consorting with my worst enemy! And in his room, not yours. If my reactions to you now are less than sensitive, I'm sorry, but the evidence was overwhelming.''

She was quiet for a moment, shocked by those admissions—first, that his threat had been a lie, and second, that he'd ''adored her.'' She couldn't help a little shudder of joy at that, then reminded herself that he'd phrased his pronouncement in the past tense. She cleared her throat.

''Well, nothing's changed,'' she said with great dignity, to hide emotions so complicated *she* didn't even understand them. ''The evidence is still the same. Why should you change your mind about it?''

''I don't know,'' he admitted, dropping his hands from her. ''Having you here again reminds me of all the good times, and it's just hard to equate that picture of you in Brian's bed with…the real you.''

She could have let the old issue go. That was a supreme admission on his part, and her acceptance of it at that point in time might have cleared that away between them. But the problem went deeper, and if this baby was ever going to have two parents in the same household, the problem had to be uprooted.

''You stopped loving me before the Brian thing ever happened.'' She folded her arms and spoke firmly, trying to make it clear they were having this out.

He looked just as firm. ''I *never* stopped loving you.''

She was rocked by his sincerity—and now more confused than ever. ''Then, what happened?''

He shrugged and shifted his weight. ''I'm not sure. I think you just…rattled my world. My father gave me big responsibilities very early in my life, and when other kids were partying in graduate school, I was learning to take over an international corporation. This, after I was completely grounded by the two anchors of my mother's defection and my sister's abduction. There couldn't be happiness for me, only work." He put both hands in his pockets and shrugged again. "Then you came along and made me happy."

Her throat tightened and fire burned behind her eyes. "For one lousy month. Then you were unhappy again. Hardly something you can hold against me for a lifetime."

"I stopped *being* happy," he corrected gently. "It had nothing to do with you."

"Then what did it have to do with?"

"Ah…guilt, I guess, that I'd managed to put those things aside and find my own personal light."

"You're entitled to that," she said, touched by his obvious pain. She stepped closer to put a hand to his arm, and as she did, she noticed Sawyer and Campbell standing in the doorway.

Killian saw them, too, and ran a hand down his face. She knew the confidences were over.

"I'm sorry," Sawyer said, stepping into the room. His tie was undone and the top button of his shirt open. He looked distressed. "We…arrived home at the same time and heard shouting in the kitchen, and wanted to make sure everything was all right."

"And stayed to listen?" Killian asked judiciously.

Campbell smiled, probably to suggest that whatever they'd heard wasn't important because they were family. "Well, you have to admit it was damn interesting stuff." Then he grew serious. "But, you're an idiot to feel guilty about Abby. I'm the one who shouted at her that day and took my toys away from her. You were always carrying her around when the rest of us had had it with her breaking our stuff."

"Oh, come on," Sawyer said. "Let's not do this now. Dad spent a fortune on therapy for all of us. He'd roll over in his grave if he knew all our lives still revolve around Abby being gone."

The telephone rang and Campbell went to answer it while the others stared at one another disconsolately.

Campbell held the receiver toward Killian. "It's Lew," he said. "Something about a trip to Florida."

"Okay." Killian was controlled again, that rare glimpse of the man inside gone. He turned to Sawyer. "Will you walk Cordie upstairs?" he asked.

Disgusted with the whole situation, she said stiffly, "I'm perfectly capable of walking upstairs by myself." And she set off to do just that.

But Sawyer caught up with her and took her arm.

She stopped to extricate her arm and assure him again that she could walk up a flight of stairs even after a loud argument, when he put a finger to his lips and recaptured her. "Shh!" he whispered. "I have to tell you something."

He ushered her up the stairs, then stopped at the doorway to her room. He leaned a shoulder against the molding and smiled gently. "I want to try to explain to you where some of Killian's guilt comes from."

"You don't have to," she said, suddenly very weary. "He feels responsible for the whole world. I see it at work all the time. He probably thinks that if he'd been home that night, Abby wouldn't—"

"Well, yeah," Sawyer agreed. "Campbell and I were both here, so you can imagine how guilty we feel. I was talking about his guilt about our mother leaving."

She nodded. "All the experts say that every child of a divorce feels responsible for the parent leaving."

Sawyer nodded with a wince. "He comes by his guilt more directly, because I blamed him and made it clear to him that it was all his fault—over and over, in fact." He shook his head at the memory. "I was terrified when she left," he said. "I mean, it isn't like we saw her that much. I was only three at the time, but I remember that we were always in the nursery, and all she did was stick her head in once in a while and wave. Yet Killian and I used to live for those moments. And in my selfish little child's mind, I couldn't believe she'd left because of anything I'd done, so it had to be Killian's fault." He made a self-deprecating face. "I was the hoodlum, mind you, and he was the Goody Two-shoes always rescuing me from trouble. Still, it made sense to me that he was to blame. And like I said, I told him that again and again."

"But you were little children," she argued urgently. "Even if he took your accusations to heart then, certainly he knows better now."

"Childhood stuff stays with you. And until I was in my teens, I was always quick to remind him that our mother's leaving was his fault just to keep myself sane. You'd think he'd have blamed me in turn, but he never did. He was always smarter and nobler than me. I resented that for a long time, but now I just accept it." He touched her lightly on the shoulder. "Good night, Cordie. I'm glad you're back."

She hugged him quickly, then went into her room. Her argument with Killian played repeatedly in her head as she shed her robe and slippers and climbed into bed. She imagined him and Sawyer as children, Sawyer blaming him for their mother's abandonment, and felt tears on her face.

But what played in her mind as she drifted off to sleep, her hand on the gentle swell of her baby, was Killian's saying with complete conviction, "I *never* stopped loving you."

Chapter Eight

This was insane, Killian told himself as he quietly turned the knob and pushed open the door into Cordie's room. It was cool and dark, and he stood there a moment to let his eyes adjust.

He caught her scent and heard her quiet breathing. Then he couldn't wait another moment, whether he could see where he was going or not. Absently, he realized that that could also apply to the way their life was going. He was tired of old grudges, tired of being doubtful, tired of holding back. It wasn't his style, and the effort was a strain.

He went quietly toward the side of the bed near the window, noticing that the digital display on her clock read 12:45. After he'd talked to Tokyo, he'd entered all the changes that had to be made in an e-mail to Lew and sent it. Then he'd walked around with a gin and tonic in his hand, trying to talk himself out of going to Cordie's room. A legion of arguments denied the wisdom of making love to her right now—she'd been correct; nothing had been solved.

Yet, deep in his heart, that didn't seem to matter.

He sat on the edge of her bed. She continued to sleep, curled up on her side, one hand wrapped around the other under her chin. He put a gentle hand to her hair. She'd freed it from the ponytail for sleeping and it was all over her pillow, strands of it lay across her face and some of it was tangled in the blankets over her shoulder.

The cat, he noticed belatedly, slept on the pillow beside her.

Cordie sat up suddenly, awakened by his touch, a gasp in her throat he suspected was about to turn into a scream. Versace leaped up on all fours, his back arching.

Killian quickly put a hand to Cordie's mouth to stifle the sound, whispering, ''Cordie, shh! It's me!''

Her shoulders slumped in relief, and as he lowered his hand, she smacked his shoulder. ''You scared me to death!'' she squeaked. ''What's the matter?'' Her expression changed to one of concern. ''Is something wrong?''

''Everything's fine,'' he reassured her quickly. ''Except between us.''

Her eyes glistened in a sudden glow of moonlight. ''I don't know what to do about it.''

He pushed her hair back over her shoulder. ''I had a thought on that.''

She was silent for an instant, then she asked softly, ''What?''

''Let's just shelve it.''

She blinked once. ''Shelve it?''

"Forget it. That's what we do with ideas we can't make work either because they don't seem to get us anywhere or they have problems that are too complicated or too costly to solve. We stop wasting time on them."

She opened her mouth to speak, as though she wanted to challenge his solution. She smiled, instead. "I'm in favor of that."

"Excellent. Then I've got something for you." He pulled her wedding ring out of the pocket of his jeans and slipped it on the third finger of her left hand. Then he put it to his lips.

She held it toward the moonlight as though needing to see that it really was her wedding ring. Her look melted his spine.

"Come with me," he said, and he scooped her into his arms and carried her across the hall to his room. "I know you love your little turret," he told her quietly as he backed up to his door and asked her to nudge it open, "but this is our room. We can turn that one into a study for you." He dropped her into the middle of his still-made bed. There was no moonlight on this side of the house, and he couldn't see her face, but he heard her little sound of surprise.

"Are you…serious?" she asked.

"Very," he replied. "Do you still want to be married to me?"

"Yes." She replied instantly.

"Because you want a father for our baby?" He had to ask.

"No." Her voice trembled but was clear. "Because I never stopped loving you, either."

That was what he'd wanted to hear, but more than he'd dared hope for. He drew his sweatshirt over his head, then unfastened his belt and his jeans. Her pajama top flew through the shadows, followed by the bottoms.

He sat down to pull off his shoes and socks. She knelt behind him and wrapped her arms around his neck, kissing his shoulder. "Killy," she whispered in his ear as she nibbled on it. "I've missed you so much."

He turned his head to catch her lips. "I love you, Cordie," he said, the words coming up out of the depths of his heart—a place he hadn't explored in a long time. "I'm sorry about everything."

"It's shelved, remember," she said. "Forgotten." She came around him to urge his upper body down to the mattress. Then she climbed off the bed, grabbed one leg of his jeans in each hand and tugged.

He lifted up on his elbows to help her, but not too much because he enjoyed watching the ivory curves of her body at work—all he could see of her in the darkness—the delicate convexity of her cheek and chin, the slight swell of their baby, rounded breasts and hips; the seductive invitation of the shadows at her throat, her waist, the juncture of thigh and torso.

The moment he was free of the jeans, he boosted himself backward, caught her hand and yanked her to him.

She came to him with a startled little laugh, her arms open and wrapping around him as he fell onto his back. The sensation of being flesh to flesh with her again made him realize how much the past few weeks had changed him.

He remembered the very first time he'd held her like this. He'd felt powerful, victorious, filled with love for her but very much aware of how her love enriched him.

This time he felt humbled, pathetically grateful, filled with love for her and just beginning to grasp how much he wanted to make up to her for the previous three months.

THE NERVES under Cordie's skin quivered as Killian's arm tightened around her waist, putting every inch of him in touch with every inch of her. One hand settled between her shoulder blades and pressed her breasts against his chest while the other shaped her hip.

She felt the strength of his manhood against her and expelled a little sigh into his mouth as he kissed her. She moaned his name softly, bending her thigh to rub it against his, tortured by his readiness for her. By hers for him.

The three months without him had seemed like an eternity. Now that she was in his arms, she felt the same wonder as the first time, along with a delicious familiarity that made her tighten her grip on him and kiss his throat. "This is like…I don't know…heaven, I guess."

She reached a hand down to touch him, his warmth and power still a surprise after all the times she dreamed of gaining this moment.

''Yes,'' he whispered hoarsely, his hand sliding along the back of her thigh, fingers reaching into her. ''Heaven.''

Time dissolved at the well-remembered intimacy. His touch was so right, so welcome, so... There just were no words for it.

The promise of pleasure began instantly; the little game of its attack and withdrawal tightened her body, narrowing her awareness so that nothing existed in the universe but his body and hers.

Then he grasped her by the waist, lifted her over him and entered her. Her moan mingled with his, and she felt the old loneliness die forever as they became one again.

He braced her hands with his as she moved on him, drawing her down to him, then tightening his grip on her hands when she arched backward. The spiral narrowed and she gripped his fingers.

Shudders spun her like a wind ornament, and she heard Killian's throaty gasp as he, too, was overtaken.

Finally spent, she fell onto him, exhausted. He turned so that they lay on their sides, and reached back to pull the coverlet over them.

''Warm enough?'' he asked, holding her close so that the spread enveloped her. ''You need a pillow?''

She snuggled into him, burrowing her nose in his throat. "I'm warm enough, and I'll just use you for a pillow."

THAT WAS FINE with him. He remembered how invincible he used to feel when this beautiful, magical woman held on to him as though he was essential to her well-being.

He hadn't realized then how essential she was to his.

He put a hand down to her stomach. "Baby okay?"

"I'm sure, because I feel wonderful."

"Yeah. Me, too." He kissed her forehead and encouraged her to sleep.

"How can I sleep," she asked on a yawn, "when what I've been dreaming of for three long months has finally been given to me?"

He kissed her soundly for that. "Well, we can't raid the refrigerator, because we're out of ice cream. Campbell and Sawyer had some after you went to bed."

"You want to talk baby names?" she asked.

"No Kaylees or Ashleys, okay? I think everybody at the office has little girls with those names. And the boys are all Jordan and Austin."

She yawned again. "I was thinking Killian or…Abigail."

He kissed her again because it was such a sweet thought. She was asleep before he could suggest an alternative to a Junior Abbott.

KILLIAN STAYED HOME the next day because it was the day before the annual meeting and he wanted to make sure the audio electronics in the great room downstairs, which would be used for all group meetings, were in good working order. And he didn't think he could be away from Cordie for an entire day.

With their love life renewed, all the old longing for her had doubled and his capacity for her tripled. He'd made love to her when she awakened him this morning at six, the cat watching them suspiciously from the desk. He felt long overdue for a dose of her already.

But she was in a working mode today. After that initial panic the day the original caterer had backed out, she'd taken control of the details of the meeting with a cheer and efficiency that even Barbara admired—and Barbara, an executive secretary for twenty-seven years, gave no quarter to anyone.

Cordie ran around in her new jeans and a blue-and-white sweatshirt with the Abbott Mills logo on it—a sheep standing atop the two L's in Mills—so that the workers setting up the pavilion, and the gardening staff manicuring the flower beds around the house, would easily recognize her.

Winfield's gaze followed her. "I could do all that," he said to Killian as Killian walked by with a cup of coffee and his notes for his welcoming speech. Winfield pointed down the sloping lawn to where the pavilion was being set up. Cordie, a clipboard in the crook of her arm, a long fiery braid down her back, was in earnest conversation with a workman. "Shouldn't she be at the store or the office? Or in her room with her feet up?"

"I put her in charge of this project," Killian explained, "to keep her out of the store, where she was too involved with unloading freight. This was supposed to be lighter work."

Winfield laughed scornfully. "Really. Well, look at that."

He pointed again to where the heavy plastic-coated canvas had been stretched out on the ground. Workers were pulling on cords and canvas to raise the pavilion's sides and Cordie was helping.

Killian swore, handed Winfield his coffee and his notes and took off out the door and down the slope.

"You don't have to help with every phase of the operation," Killian said, holding her hand and dragging her with him back up the slope. "A good manager learns to direct things."

She frowned at him. "You don't manage that way. You're always in the middle of what's going on."

"I'm not four months pregnant."

On the porch off the library and overlooking the garden, Kezia had set up a table with pastries, fruit and coffee for the workmen, and Killian led Cordie there now.

Cordie went to a hot pot filled with water and selected a tea bag out of a small bowl while Killian took an orange and poured himself a cup of coffee.

Kezia had scored the orange in four from stem to bottom, simplifying the peeling process.

They went to a bench in the garden and sat. She bit into an apple fritter while he pulled the peeled orange in half, removed a section and popped it in his mouth.

As she ate, she told him she'd talked to the caterer that morning and he'd asked her what she thought of adding marinated vegetables to the lunch menu for Saturday. She'd shrewdly consulted Kezia, who approved the idea.

"She's taking this all very well," she said, after chewing another bite of fritter. "I expected her to be all upset with strangers invading her kitchen, but she—" Then she made an odd sound like a vacuum sucking air. She put a hand over her mouth and her eyes above it grew huge.

"What?" he demanded, putting his orange and cup down on the small table in front of them, convinced she was choking.

She held up the fritter in her hand. "I'm eating an apple fritter!" she exclaimed. "Look!"

He needed a moment to grasp the importance of that.

"Yeah?"

She put a hand to her stomach, her eyes unfocused as though she was analyzing something. "I'm not nauseous," she said in quiet wonder. "I'm not even queasy!" She threw her arms around him, laughing. "I'm over the morning sickness!"

He had to laugh with her. He hadn't been sure

how much longer he could stand to watch her eat ice cream for every meal. Not that an apple fritter was a better choice, but it was staying down and that presented her with all kinds of new options.

Then he was completely distracted from his thoughts by the fact that he was holding her in his arms—not to offer comfort, but because she was genuinely happy about something and spontaneously chose to share the moment with him.

He felt the taut roundness of her breasts against his chest, the silkiness of her arm against the side of his face, the strength of her grip on him. Her laughter rippled in his ear and her hair smelled of her favorite apple and herb shampoo.

He wanted her so desperately he couldn't stand it another moment. He turned to Winfield, who wandered around, hands in his pockets, looking for something to do.

"Want to watch over things for a couple of hours?" he asked.

Winfield appeared delighted, though his dignity remained intact. "Of course, Mr. Abbott."

"Good. Mrs. Abbott and I are going to town for lunch."

Winfield frowned at his watch. "But it's only ten-thirt—" he began, then, suddenly seeing something new in their faces this morning, he smiled, instead. "Take your time."

"Where are we really going?" Cordie asked as he put her into the Jaguar.

"To the boathouse," he replied, waving at Kezia,

who was replenishing the refreshments table, "then we are going to town for lunch."

They used to run to the boathouse for privacy when there was too much happening at the house. He could see in her eyes that she supported the plan.

THE WORLD had been restored to Cordie the night before when Killian told her he wanted to begin again, and it was painted with color today when they made love on the old bed usually reserved for sleeping when fishing trips required really early rising.

Sun streamed through blue-and-red rough-woven curtains and lent the old wooden beams and floor a silky luster. Birds sang, water lapped around the little house and the workmen could be heard in the yard shouting instructions to one another and laughing.

She'd dreamed of Killian wanting her again, and now that he did, the possibility of her dreams coming true was almost alarming. She'd had the perfect life once before and lost it through no real fault of her own. Was it safe to slip into that comfortable confidence that life with Killian made her feel? Or was she just making herself vulnerable?

As he kissed her soundly one last time before rolling off her and handing her her clothes, then pulling on his own, she decided that life was *about* being vulnerable. And if she didn't believe him when he said he was putting the past away, how could she expect him to believe her?

Yes. That was logical. Scary, but logical.

"Where do you want to go for lunch?" he asked as he pointed the car toward town.

"Fulio's," she said instantly.

He cast her a doubtful glance. "You're sure your stomach can take that?"

She nodded. "I'm invincible! I can eat again."

"Okay. I hope you're right."

Losthampton was a picturesque little place full of antique shops, clothing stores, food stands and some of the island's nicest restaurants. The population of twelve hundred swelled to four or five thousand residents in the summer and many more tourists just passing through.

It was June and the invasion had already begun, but they were still able to find a table at Fulio's, a quaint Italian place that served wonderful fresh salads and flavorful pasta dishes.

The owner, a cheerful bearded man with a white kitchen towel wrapped around his waist, greeted them eagerly.

"Killian! I haven't seen you since…since…" Obviously unwilling to say "since Cordie left," he sidetracked by wrapping his arms around her. "How nice to see you back!" He held her away from him and looked from one to the other. "You *are* back?"

"I'm back, Fulio," she said, patting her stomach. "And we're expecting in October."

There were exclamations in Italian, more hugs, then he led them to their favorite table in the back near a tall, spindly potted palm.

"Pasta putanesca!" Cordie ordered firmly when a young waiter came to take their order.

Killian frowned at her across the table. "Cordie, are you really sure you're up to sardines and capers? I mean, many people find those indigestible, even without—"

"Pasta putanesca!" she repeated. "And Caesar salad—no croutons. And is there tiramisu today?"

The waiter, jotting madly to keep up with her, nodded.

"Good. Can you save us two pieces?"

"Just save one piece," Killian corrected. "And I'll have pasta primavera, Caesar salad and I'll have her croutons." He leaned toward her as the waiter walked away. "Are you eating for three? Or four?"

She spread both hands as though the possibility could exist. "Who knows? I've been hungry for months and I've finally got my appetite back. And I'm at Fulio's!" She looked around her in delight and he found himself infected with her enthusiasm.

This was how he went down before, he recalled. She made him happy, made him forget, caught him in her vortex of cheer and fun and left him wondering what the hell he was doing.

But he was strangely fearless this time. This was living, he now knew. He hadn't done a lot of that before she'd danced into his life or after she'd left it.

He could feel his pulse thrumming again, blood moving in his veins, his heart beating to some cosmic tempo he lost the sound of when she wasn't around.

"How can you not want tiramisu?" she asked, reaching across the table to weave her fingers into his. Her eyes sparkled. "You can have a bite of mine."

He squeezed her fingers. "That's very generous."

"I love you," she said softly.

He drew her hand to his lips and kissed her knuckles. "I love you, too."

She ate every bite of her salad, her pasta putanesca and all but one bite of the tiramisu she insisted that he taste.

The food was delicious, but he found it more of a sensory thrill to watch her eat—rolling her eyes, making sounds of pleasure, licking her lips—than eating it himself.

After lunch, they headed back to the car and stopped halfway across the lot. Cordie drew in her breath in a strangled gasp and Killian just froze for a moment, collecting himself, getting a virulent anger under control before he took another step.

Brian Girard leaned against the white Jaguar, arms folded, long legs stretched out before him, obviously waiting.

Chapter Nine

Cordie finally understood what was generating that dormant fear. Somehow, she'd known there'd be another showdown between Killian and Brian.

Cordie had met Brian Girard in college when they'd worked together on sets and costumes for junior- and senior-class theatrical productions at Columbia. She'd thought him intelligent and witty, but she'd never dated him because he had a tendency to drink too much.

She suspected that the drinking came about because his father was a critical tyrant for whom Brian could never measure up. She'd wondered if it was because he was adopted and lacked his father's lethal instincts, though he seemed to like the world of business.

Brian seldom complained about his father's attitude, but she'd witnessed an episode on a parents' weekend when his mother's graciousness had been unable to cover his father's rudeness. He'd made it clear he had better things to do.

Still, Brian was clever and hardworking, and he

and Cordie had developed a friendship over the long nights of designing and painting sets and making costumes. While she sewed, he created swords, shields and other props used onstage. They often shared pizza or Chinese food and went for coffee when they were finished for the night.

They'd run into each other fairly regularly since their school days because of their parallel career paths. He'd joined the November Corporation, which owned the Parisienne stores, an internationally known chain of fine department stores, and she'd bought women's wear for Bloomford's. In his capacity as marketing director, he'd often turned up at the same markets and shows she attended.

His attempts to take her out had continued and she'd continued to decline, though he seemed to be over the drinking problem. He'd taken her refusals good-naturedly, and she'd hoped that what had happened in that Paris hotel had somehow been an accident.

But he'd admitted to her before that he knew her husband and that they'd disliked each other most of their lives. They'd become serious enemies the day Brian had joined his father's business. He was as determined as his father to destroy Abbott Mills.

Cordie suspected that the grudge ran deeper than business. And it certainly did look as though he'd planned to be in her room the moment Killian appeared.

As she studied him now, leaning negligently against the car, moving slowly to straighten when he caught sight of them, she found it hard to detect any animosity. Thick shouldered and slim-hipped in gray slacks and a pale blue sweater, his blond good looks burnished by the sun, he smiled, as though he waited to greet friends.

She put her hand on Killian's arm, feeling the bristling vibrations coming from him. She hoped it indicated simple alertness.

He started walking toward the car.

"Hey, you two," Brian said as they reached him. "I was dropping off some paperwork at my father's. He's working at home today. And I was surprised to see the car at Fulio's, then I remembered that Dad told me the two of you were back together."

Cordie, trying to fortify her union with Killian in Brian's eyes, said brightly, "We're expecting in October."

"October," Brian repeated, apparently thinking. She didn't know what he was doing and remained clueless even when he asked, "Mmm. When in October?"

"The seventeenth," she replied.

He nodded and turned to Killian with a determination to hurt in his eyes that was crystal clear despite the smile. "No question that it's yours, then."

She finally understood that he'd been counting back to the hotel-room incident.

Killian's fist shot out so fast she didn't even see the move coming. Cordie screamed. Brian's upper body snapped back with the violence of the blow. Killian set her back, out of harm's way, preparing for a return punch, but Brian simply straightened, took a handkerchief out of his pocket and put it to a bloody lip, hatred for Killian in his eyes, and something else she couldn't quite read. It was almost…guilt. Or sadness. But that didn't make sense.

"Not a bad punch for a guy who never works out," Brian said.

"The fact that I don't do it at a trendy gym doesn't mean I don't do it," Killian replied. Then he added darkly, "Get away from my car."

Brian stepped away, still dabbing at his lip.

Killian put Cordie in the passenger seat, then turned to Brian. "Stay out of my life," he said. "And don't come near Cordie unless you want to spend the next fifty years hooked up to life support." Then he walked around the car, climbed in behind the wheel and drove away with a roar of the Jaguar's powerful engine.

CORDIE SAT QUIETLY, her eyes closed, most of the way home. Brian had effectively murdered the beautiful mood that had existed between her and Killian and sent her husband to that dark place men go to whenever violence erupts between them.

He didn't say an angry word to her, but his foot on the accelerator was heavy while his hands controlled the car with tense but perfect accuracy. His brain worked on what he was doing, but he himself was elsewhere.

"I'm sorry," she said finally, opening her eyes and watching the familiar road pass.

"For what?" he asked. She felt him glance at her and met his eyes.

"For being something he can use to get to you."

He shook his head, shifting down as they came up behind a slow truck. "That's shelved, remember?"

"He just brought it right out again. And it'll never go away unless you believe me. That's why you're not talking to me about it now."

"I believe you." He passed the truck and picked up speed. "I don't need to talk about it anymore."

"Then why did you hit him?"

"Because it was a nasty thing to say, and he deserves to be punched around for wasting a good life on petty jealousies and taking out his neuroses on people he's jealous of."

She waited a moment, wondering if he'd even be receptive to the notion that something else was going on with Brian. "Did you notice his eyes?" she asked finally.

He shook his head once. "I was aiming at his mouth."

"His father thinks he's a loser," she said, preparing to launch a case for blaming his behavior on personal problems.

Killian sent her a glance that told her not to waste her time. "Please. He's a grown man. Your life is your life and you deal with it. Begrudging other people their successes and trying to diminish them because you were too busy playing around to accomplish the same things is small."

To argue with that assessment of Brian's behavior would be hard, so she gave up her efforts to gain sympathy for him.

At home again, she had to force herself to get involved with the project at hand and ignore her uneasiness about Brian. She went to arbitrate a dispute between Winfield and the man in charge of putting up the pavilions.

"It doesn't look secure," Winfield insisted of one of the smaller pavilions, intended to display the new Abbott Woman winter line. "If this is going to hold clothes and the whole thing falls down, dumping the clothes in the grass, Mr. Abbott will be out a lot of money."

Cordie loved the way Winfield worried not only about every person in the household but every dime the Abbotts made. He was careful to be sure that nothing in the house was ever wasted.

"I'm telling you, it's secure," the other man insisted.

"And I'm telling you I saw you put it up," Winfield said, "and it isn't."

"We have a contract with his company," Cordie told Winfield. "If the pavilion collapses and ruins the clothes, we'll sue. So I'm sure he was careful."

The man from the rental company swallowed and walked away.

Winfield smiled at Cordie with new respect. "Well done, Mrs. Abbott," he said.

That was high praise indeed.

Cordie headed for the house to check on the caterers and walked through the great room to see what progress was being made on setting it up for the big inside meetings.

Killian and two electricians were sitting in the middle of the floor, drinking coffee and discussing someone's batting average. She caught Killian's eye as she passed and he winked at her, seeming none the worse for his experience with Brian. The memory of Brian's cruel remark and Killian's angry reaction still lay like a pall over her day.

She suspected that was because she didn't think his problem with Brian was going to end there. Killian claimed to put no credibility in Brian's remark, but she couldn't help wondering if somewhere deep inside—perhaps even unconsciously—he really did.

She felt on edge and uncertain as she went over menus, folded programs, made information packets for everyone attending. The folders included Abbott Mills's history, information on all its various companies and products, its annual report and a T-shirt with the Abbott Mills logo.

She didn't stop until dinnertime.

She'd headed upstairs to take a quick shower before dinner, when she halted in her tracks, a very subtle fluttering in her stomach. She stood still, waiting for another flutter.

Killian, just coming out of his bedroom, came to her worriedly. "The pasta putanesca fighting back?"

She shook her head and shushed him with a finger to her lips. He waited.

"The baby," she whispered.

"Why are we whispering?" he asked, also in a whisper. "Is he sleeping?"

She gave him a reproving look. "I thought I felt movement."

"No kidding." He put an arm around her shoulders and the flat of his other hand on her stomach.

"I doubt you'll be able to feel anything," she warned softly. "I barely did. But I'm pretty sure that was what it was. Or I'm gestating butterflies."

He grinned and kissed her. "I'll bet it was the pasta. Lew says you don't feel anything until the middle of the fifth month."

She raised her eyebrows in a superior gesture. "Maybe Karen doesn't, but we're having a genius."

He laughed lightly. "Really. You didn't tell me that."

"It was going to be a surprise. But you may as well be warned, our child will be doing everything early."

"Well, I don't want him showing up at board meetings until he's potty-trained."

That was the second time he'd referred to the baby as "he." "You won't be disappointed if it's a girl, will you?" she asked. "I mean, a girl could carry on the company. I could have done it for my father if I'd loved furniture as much as I do fashion."

"I'm so happy the baby's coming," he said, squeezing her shoulders, "that the gender doesn't matter. I just think in terms of 'he.'"

"Well, I'm thinking in terms of 'she.'"

"I'm also thinking in terms of dinner," he said,

pushing her gently toward the room. "Hurry up. You don't want to be responsible for keeping Sawyer and Campbell from their food, believe me."

She pointed to her little turret across the hall. "But my clothes are in—"

"No, they're not. Kezia moved them into my room." He smiled wryly. "We had to put my clothes in the bathroom to make room for yours, but marriage is all about compromise."

She liked that he'd moved her things, liked that he was teasing her. It made the Brian episode less affecting.

KILLIAN WENT into the library to call Lew and was surprised to find Campbell sitting in a leather chair near the French doors. He was staring thoughtfully, legs stretched in front of him, arms dangling over the arms of the chair.

"Rough day?" Killian asked, certain something troubled him.

"No, good day." Campbell straightened and indicated the chair opposite. "Can you sit for a minute?"

Killian went to join him, feeling wary but concealing it with an expectant look. "Yeah?"

"I got a callback at Flamingo Gables," Campbell announced. "They'd like me there this weekend. I know I promised I'd help with the annual meeting, but I—"

Killian dismissed any need to explain with a wave

of his hand. "That's all right. But…you *got* the job and they want you there this weekend?"

Campbell shook his head. "It's down to two of us. The other guy worked for a movie star in one of those tiny valleys in Southern California. More grounds, but less going on."

"So you have a good chance."

"I think so."

Killian hated things he couldn't fix, but Campbell had to find whatever it was he was searching for. And it didn't seem to be here.

"Anything I can do for you? Drive you to the airport? What time?"

Campbell pushed himself to his feet and Killian stood with him. "Billie's flying me down, but she can't land the 'copter with pavilions all over the place." He paused to grin. "So I'm supposed to meet her at the airport. You stay with Cordie. Daniel will drive me."

"Okay. Do you have time for dinner first?"

"Yeah. I'm not meeting her until eight." Campbell shifted his weight, looking slightly uncomfortable. It was his bad-news or painful-concession face. And he'd already delivered the bad news. "I'm glad you understand," Campbell added in a rush. "I mean, I need to do this, but I know Mom's going to freak, and Sawyer doesn't get it at all, even though he's acting like he's happy to get rid of me. Kezia's glaring at me, too. So…thank you for being on my side."

"Sure." Killian put an arm around his shoulders as they walked together toward the door.

Sawyer stood in the doorway, arms folded, a satisfied expression aimed at Campbell. "We're going to put a pool table in your room," he said. "And find a way to get your inheritance from you."

Campbell rolled his eyes at Killian. "See what you can do about him while I wash my hands for dinner." He pushed Sawyer aside and left the room.

Killian and Sawyer watched Campbell lope down the hall to the stairs.

"You were very generous and understanding," Sawyer said.

Killian sighed, unable to dispel a sense of sadness. "I didn't mean it," he admitted.

Sawyer glanced at him a second time and apparently caught the grim acceptance he'd hidden from Campbell. He gave him a fraternal clap on the shoulder. "Cheer up. You've still got me."

"Yeah," Killian replied flatly. "That's a lot of my problem." He'd started in the direction of the dining room, when Sawyer stopped him.

"Wait!" he said with sudden urgency. "I came here to talk to you."

Killian groaned and turned back into the room. "If you tell me you're leaving, I'll murder you. Painfully."

"No such luck." Sawyer had a variation on Campbell's bad-news–painful-concession expression. It was a glance away, followed by a frown at the floor, then a challenging look into Killian's eyes.

He did it when he was embarrassed because he very seldom was and didn't know how to deal with the feeling.

He wore that face now. Killian folded his arms and waited.

"When we were kids," Sawyer began, his forehead pleated as he thought back. "I used to…blame you for Mom leaving."

Killian took a moment to readjust his brain for old, personal stuff rather than the new ways Sawyer had found to complicate his life.

"Yeah," he said.

Sawyer squinted into his eyes. "You know I was an idiot, right, and didn't have a clue what I was talking about?"

Killian concealed his surprise. "I've always realized you were an idiot, yes."

Sawyer accepted that with a grin. "Good. Because though you put a lot of stock in what I say about the foundation, I'd hate to think you took any of *that* stuff to heart."

"You were a little kid."

"I blamed you until we were in high school."

Killian remembered that clearly, but he hadn't minded all that much, since he'd been convinced he was probably to blame, too. But Sawyer didn't need any more guilt than both of them already suffered. He shrugged. "Don't worry. You were an idiot then, too."

Sawyer gave him a knowing look. "You don't have to be heroic with me. You're only two years older and we went through all of this together. I experienced firsthand how much it hurt. But we've got to let it go. We didn't pick a selfish mother, and there's nothing we could have done about Abby. But we lucked out with Chloe, and Campbell's not half-bad if you can ignore that earnest, personal-search crap.''

"Moving on is important to him."

"I get that. I just wish he understood he's important to us."

"He'll get it eventually."

"Okay, well…" Sawyer was apparently finished being serious. "I just didn't want to be responsible for any guilt you might be feeling that's keeping you from being happy with Cordie."

"I am happy."

"The two of you looked as though you'd had a fight when you returned from town."

"Wasn't that," Killian corrected. "When we came out of the restaurant, Brian Girard was leaning on my car. He made a rude remark about the baby and I hit him."

Sawyer's eyes widened. "You did? Wow. Good going. I didn't know you had violence in you." Then he scrutinized Killian's face as though searching for injury. "Did you knock him out first punch?"

Killian shook his head as he pulled the door open again. "No. But he didn't hit me back."

"That's weird."

"Yeah, well, that seems to have been his M.O. most of his life. Doesn't have much use for you and

Campbell, either, but he loves to harass me. He hates to lose to me, yet he appears to enjoy putting himself in my way.''

''Has something to prove, I guess. Like the big dogs.''

Killian smiled thinly. ''Cordie claims he has issues with his father. That the old man's never thought he measured up and makes him feel small.''

''Girard is a demanding old man.''

''Yeah. But if we have to get over Mom and Abby, Brian should have to get over the old man.''

''True. But we have each other. He doesn't have anybody.''

''Yeah.'' Still, Killian was in no mood to feel sympathy for Brian Girard. He took off in the direction of the dining room and Sawyer followed.

After dinner, Killian, Cordie and Sawyer waved Campbell off as he sat in the front of the limo with Daniel, and offered their good wishes.

When the limo was out of sight, Cordie moved between the men, hooked an arm in each of theirs. ''You're such a couple of liars,'' she said, and urged them back inside.

Chapter Ten

The house was cheerfully chaotic the following morning when the chartered bus arrived with the thirty staff members attending the annual meeting, together with Barbara and the four secretaries conscripted to assist her and Cordie.

The third floor, once the nursery, had been converted years ago to seven good-size bedrooms. One had been set up dormitory style to hold the four secretaries, and everyone else had signed up to bunk in pairs and threes.

Sawyer volunteered to sleep in the boathouse since he would be practicing this year's fund-raising stunt for the foundation much of the weekend. That left his room and Campbell's empty. Those and the tower room provided more space on the second floor.

Cordie had suggested to Killian that they move downstairs into the gym, but he'd insisted that she be comfortable. Charmed by his thoughtfulness, she didn't argue.

She stood with Killian to greet guests at the door,

with Barbara behind them, distributing packets. The secretaries guided all the arrivals to their rooms.

"If textiles and fashion ever fail us," Cordie said to Killian between guests, "we can go into the hotel business."

She could have bitten her tongue the moment the words were out of her mouth. Mentioning hotels considering their last meeting in one, was tempting their new rapport.

But he didn't notice. "I worked the desk in a hotel in Southhampton one summer during high school. I even have experience. And if you introduce the bellmen to girls, they'll share their tips."

"Important insider information."

"That's what getting ahead's all about." He slanted her a grin. "As long as you don't buy stock based on that tip." Then he turned his attention to the door as new arrivals walked up the front steps.

The welcome meeting had a note of cheerful camaraderie as everyone gathered in the great room with doughnuts and coffee. In preference to folding chairs, there were side chairs, occasional chairs, slipper chairs, every kind of chair commandeered from other parts of the house. Some guests were already wearing their T-shirts, and several had put them on over their clothes.

Conversation was deafening by the time Killian stood near the fireplace to get everyone's attention. Silence fell as he stood in front of the group.

He spoke clearly, quietly, and with a sense of humor that maintained the smiles with which all had come into the room. He told them that since they'd worked so hard for him, he wanted to show his gratitude by bringing them to his home.

''We're going to pick your brains,'' he said, ''help you learn about new products, feed you well, take you on a tour of Shepherd's Knoll and Losthampton and help you rest well, so that the next fiscal year will be as productive as this one has been. And because we've had such a banner year, it's my pleasure to start our weekend by announcing a ten percent raise for administrative staff across the board.''

There was astonishment, then raucous cheering as they all turned to one another in unashamedly greedy delight.

''And when you go back to work on Monday,'' he added, ''you can tell your employees the hourly rate of the rank and file goes up, too, effective July 1.'' More cheering.

''Now that I have you in a positive frame of mind,'' he said with a smile, ''look in your packets for the orange Ideas page, and I'll tell you what we'd like you to do with that over the next few days.''

Cordie, leaning against the doorway to the hallway, watched the crowd of smiling, whispering employees leafing through their packets and knew this annual meeting was already a success.

While Killian conducted a tour of the house and grounds, Barbara and the secretaries stocked the pavilion outside for the next session—a get-acquainted program involving memory games, followed by a quiz about the company, with prizes for the winner.

Cordie went into the kitchen to see how the preparations for lunch were going. Versace, she noticed, was sitting in a corner, gobbling cubed chicken. He'd been exploring the house lately, and Kezia was the only member of the household he treated with any respect. Probably because she provided food.

Kezia, who'd been a brick while the caterers had invaded her domain, now seemed to be losing it. Her eyes and nose were red as she gave Cordie a glare and pointed a thumb over her shoulder toward Jack Eagan, the refined Englishman who'd hired Cordie. He nibbled on a skewer of fruit while inspecting a tray of small pastries.

"At home," he said, "when I was in service to the duke of Burrage, we'd put each of the pastries in its own crenellated paper cup."

Kezia smiled grimly at Cordie. "At home you were serving the gentry," she said, raising her voice so Jack would hear her without her having to turn around. "Here we have just a lot of hungry people who care less about how a pastry looks than how easy it is to grab."

Over Kezia's shoulder, she saw Jack stiffen judiciously. "I assure you Mr. Abbott's staff are not a bunch of ruffians."

"Aren't you supposed to be on the tour, Jack?" Cordie asked gently, hoping to remove him from Kezia's kitchen before blood was imminently shed.

He smiled and shook his head. "Thank you, but Mr. Abbott promised me a personal tour this afternoon."

"Ah." She patted Kezia's shoulder. "I just came to see if you have everything you need."

"I forgot to pick up my allergy prescription yesterday," she said in a thick voice. "And Daniel's on an errand to the city for Mr. Abbott. Would you mind if I asked Winfield…?"

"I'll get it for you," Cordie volunteered; then, suddenly inspired, she pointed furtively in Jack's direction. "Jack, I have to get something in town. Do you want to come and see Losthampton?"

He smiled. "Thank you, but I did when we drove through on our way here. It seems patterned after a hundred little villages where I come from."

Cordie bit back laughter as she shrugged her defeat at Kezia. Kezia threatened her with the knife with which she frosted a cake.

Cordie, used to riding into town in the back of the limo, hadn't driven in weeks. She was surprised to find herself excited at the prospect.

But when she got to the garage, her small import was blocked in by Killian's Jaguar. She studied the white car dubiously. When they were first married, he'd let her drive the vehicle, but it had made him nervous. She'd thought it charming then that he was so controlled in every respect, but he worried about his car.

Asking him now was out of the question because at the moment he was leading the group toward the knoll that overlooked the beach. They were clustered around him, apparently fascinated by their surroundings and hanging on his every word.

Assuring herself that he couldn't possibly object to the half-hour trip, she ran back upstairs to get the extra set of keys he kept in an inlaid cherry-wood box on the dresser. Then she grabbed a sweater to put on over her cotton shirt and hurried back to the Jaguar.

She felt like Grace Kelly in *To Catch a Thief,* racing along that Monaco road, scarf flying out behind her. Well, she herself didn't have a scarf, but she'd freed her hair, and the wind in it was exhilarating. The day was sunny and bright, the air fragrant and intoxicating. It helped her put yesterday and Killian's confrontation with Brian to the back of her mind.

She so enjoyed being back at Shepherd's Knoll, but the last week of planning and worry about the meeting had left little time for simple relaxation. Of course, life with Killian would never allow for much of that anyway, which made moments like this all the more valuable.

She went to the drugstore for Kezia's prescription and ran into Fulio, who was buying aspirin. He smiled widely at her. "I guess we'll be seeing all your employees tonight. Your husband booked thirty-two for dinner. Prime rib and prawns."

She nodded. "He told me. And we're all looking forward to it."

He leaned toward her conspiratorially. "I'm throwing in tiramisu for dessert."

She hugged him. "Bless you!" she said.

She went back to the car, fully intending to drive

right back home, when she spotted Hudson River Ice Cream across the street and felt a desperate yearning for an ice-cream fix. She hadn't had any in two whole days.

Deciding that the five-minute delay wouldn't hurt anything because Killian had everything under control at the house with the help of Barbara and the secretaries, and Kezia and the caterers were in good form, she went in and asked for a scoop of coffee ice cream topped by a scoop of barber-pole. She sat on a bench outside the shop to enjoy the ice cream and think about what a miracle it was that her plot was working so quickly.

Killian was everything she remembered in the man she'd fallen in love with even more deeply. He'd had all his vulnerabilities locked up tightly before and been unwilling to admit that he needed her. Their life had been all about what he wanted to do for her.

She suspected that the knowledge that he was becoming a father was finally pushing the tragedies of his childhood away so that he could look ahead with hope.

She was imagining all the things she wanted the three of them to do together when a bright red Porsche pulled into the parking lot. She paid little attention—expensive sports cars were the norm around there—until a tall, fair-haired man unfolded from it, smiled at her from behind a pair of sunglasses, then strode toward her.

It was Brian Girard.

He inspired a sense of sadness in her rather than anger.

She stood and started for the Jaguar.

Brian stopped her with a hand on her arm. She shook it off and looked him in the eye. "Don't touch me," she ordered quietly. "I haven't forgotten that remark you made yesterday."

He dropped his hand from her, accepting her rebuke with a nod. He seemed repentant. "I know. I saw the car and came to apologize."

"You're spending a lot of time driving around Long Island," she said, "for Corbin Girard's marketing director."

He smiled grimly. "I'm unemployed as of last Friday. I wasn't delivering papers to my father yesterday. I was moving into my grandmother's place down the beach."

Cordie had heard that the stately old lady had died in her sleep just before Christmas.

"I'm buying the little general store between here and East Hampton."

She stared at him for a full five seconds before she could take that in.

"But I thought you loved the November Corporation. I thought you had big dreams for—"

He shook his head and interrupted. "Not anymore. My father and I can't come together on anything. He's always going to be a pirate at heart, and I...I've got other plans."

She still couldn't believe he had apology on his mind. She'd grown up with many privileged heirs to fortunes and the last thing many of them wanted to do was go into the family business. But Brian had been excited about it and eager to make his own contributions to the future of the corporation. She couldn't imagine why his father didn't appreciate that.

"Well," she said with a sigh, sorry for the unhappy state of his life when hers was going so well. "I wish you luck, but please stay out of my life."

"I will," he agreed. "But first you have to take a message to Killian for me."

"Brian," she said impatiently, certain the message was a curse or a profanity of some kind.

He raised a hand to stop her. "Just tell him not to buy those Florida Shops his stepmother's been thinking about acquiring."

When she expressed surprise that he knew that, he shrugged. "The intelligence firm my father has checking out Abbott Mills is aware of everything going on in the business. I know Chloe once worked with Celia Marsh, the owner and principal designer. What she doesn't know is that her daughter, Bridget, is the brains behind the designs. She just let her mother take the credit because she hates the limelight."

"How do you know that?"

He smiled blandly. "I dated Bridget last summer when I was on vacation."

"But…Killian will be smart enough to find that out and make sure Bridget comes with the deal."

Brian shook his head. "Mother and daughter have

an agreement to keep their collaboration secret. And Bridget's sweet on your old pal André McGinty. When the stores sell, she's moving to his camp."

She frowned at him. "After your nasty remark about the baby being Killian's, why should you care if he makes a bad business deal or not?"

Brian studied her for a moment, looked away, then back again with an indeterminate shrug. "Even the worst villain has a spark of fairness. Just tell him my father's hoping he'll buy them because it'll give him just the chink he needs to start plucking away at Abbott Mills."

Cordie sighed over the problems Killian faced on every front of his life. "Why does your father have such hostility toward the Abbotts? And don't tell me it's only business. You hate him, too. And business doesn't usually get that personal."

He thought about that a moment, then shook his head. "I don't hate anybody. Requires too much energy. And all I can say about my father is that he holds grudges forever. Tell Killian what I said."

Then he climbed into his Porsche and backed out onto the road.

Cordie wondered what to do as she drove home. She hated to think what Killian's reaction would be to learning that she'd had a conversation with Brian Girard. She'd volunteered to go to town for Kezia, but it would look as though she'd planned to meet Brian. Her newfound happiness with Killian was a wonderful but somewhat fragile thing, and she was afraid of shattering it.

Maybe she could get the message about the Florida Shops to Killian in another way.

At the house, everyone was eating on blankets opened out on the lawn. Lunch was a magnificent array of elegant cold cuts and cheeses, crab, clams and oysters on ice, and four tantalizing salads.

She hurried inside to give Kezia her prescription, then went out again to help herself to an apple-cranberry-walnut concoction on greens with a raspberry vinaigrette.

Killian came up beside her with an empty plate.

"Assure me that my car's in one piece," he said, reaching for a salad sprinkled with mortadella and provolone.

She turned to him with a look of innocence. "Of course it's in one piece. It's wrapped around a tree, but it is in one piece."

He threatened her with the salad tongs. "I'm going to presume, since you seem unscathed and even remarkably beautiful today, that the devil woman in you is teasing me."

She jabbed him with her elbow. "Your precious Jag is fine. I just ran into town to pick up a prescription for Kezia, stopped to get an ice cream, and came right back." She felt a twinge of guilt at her sin of omission.

"Good." He added a slice of cheese to his plate and pointed toward an apple tree on the far edge of the lawn. "Come and sit with me. Here, I'll carry your plate if you'll snag a couple of sodas for us."

She took two plastic glasses and extracted soft

drinks from a bucket of ice. Then she followed him across the lawn, smiling and greeting employees clustered in groups and enjoying the quiet, sunny moment.

"It's all going very well so far," she observed.

"Seems to be. I—" He stopped when one of the secretaries rushed toward them with a blanket.

"Thank you, Elizabeth," he said in pleased surprise. "But you don't have to take care of us, just our guests."

"Happy to serve you, Mr. Abbott," she answered, a dreamy quality in her raspy voice and her wide hazel eyes. She was small and doll-like and had stared at Killian since she'd arrived. Cordie felt a virulent surge of jealousy.

"Thank you," she replied for both of them. "I'll take it from here."

Elizabeth eventually swung her eyes toward Cordie, clearly surprised to see her there. "Oh. Yes. Of course. Call me if you need anything else."

When Elizabeth was out of earshot, Cordie turned to Killian with pursed lips. "You've made a conquest," she accused.

He shrugged negligently as he twisted the top off the pop and poured cola into their two glasses. "That's what I do. Corporate giants and beautiful women all succumb to my will."

"Ha-ha," she said, taking her glass from him.

He toasted her with his. "I know. Jealousy isn't funny, is it?"

She opened her mouth to deny that she was jealous, but knew she'd be lying. And she was sure he did, too. For the first time, she gave serious thought to how he must have felt when he'd walked into her hotel room and found Brian there. At the time, she'd been so focused on her own innocence and his stubborn refusal to believe it.

That had been a much more compromising situation than Elizabeth's simple adoration, yet Cordie felt as though she wanted to shake the girl until her teeth rattled and send her away. She had a sudden and clearer understanding of his feelings.

Which made approaching the Florida Shops issue that much more difficult. She could not tell him the message came from Brian.

"Are you sure the Florida Shops are a good idea?" she asked without preamble. Cursing herself for not having thought through her approach a little longer, she wasn't surprised when he turned to her with a frown. The leaves rustling in the trees shadowed his face in new ways, doing amazing things to the blue of his eyes.

"What brought that up?" he asked, fork poised over his salad.

Explain that without tripping all over yourself. "I heard some of the employees talking," she said, then forked a bite of her salad so that she could keep her gaze on her plate.

"I wasn't aware anyone knew I'd sent Lew's assistant to Florida."

She put the bite in her mouth, chewed and swallowed, playing for time.

"Word gets out. His secretary probably mentioned to someone that she'd purchased tickets to Florida for someone on his staff. Or maybe his wife told someone."

He raised an eyebrow in an indication that either was a possibility. She drew an even breath.

"Who mentioned it?" he asked.

She shrugged. "Ah…I overheard it in a group of people standing behind me this morning when everyone was milling around in the great room. I don't know who was talking about it. I just wondered if you've checked out the Florida Shops in detail yet."

When he still seemed perplexed, she smiled directly at him. "I'm just trying to prove that I'm no longer frivolous. I'm paying attention to business."

KILLIAN LEANED forward to kiss her, raspberry vinaigrette on her lips and all. He hated the thought that he'd made her feel she had to have business on her mind all the time.

"We're still checking out the Florida Shops," he said. "I sent one of Lew's people down to look at the group. But I don't want to talk about this over lunch. You're welcome to forget business and be frivolous."

"But we're holding a three-day meeting."

"Which is supposed to be about relaxing, getting better acquainted…"

"And learning more about the company, its procedures and its products so that we're all better able to work together. I'm trying to do my part.''

"Well, stop," he ordered gently. "I've got a brief break here. I'd like you to focus on being my lover."

She grinned, the urgency in her eyes quieting as she leaned into him. "In front of all these employees?"

"In deference to their sensibilities, just tell me about your plans for me later this evening, when everyone's gone to bed." He kissed her lightly. "And be specific."

Chapter Eleven

Killian had chartered a bus to take everyone to Fulio's. The atmosphere inside reminded Cordie of trips to football games when she was in high school. She and Killian and Lew and Jack sat on the bench seat in the back and joined in the songfest of the staff.

John Crowder, the director of research and development, was a man in his mid-sixties who'd been with the company for thirty years. He sang in his church's choir and had a preference for the sixties tunes of his youth. He was leading the group in a medley of old Beatles songs and they were in the middle of a loud and heartfelt rendition of "Hard Day's Night," when the bus pulled up in front of Fulio's. Everyone remained seated long enough to finish the refrain. Then they erupted in laughter and piled off the bus, to wait at the restaurant's front doors for Killian to lead the way in.

He ushered Cordie in first, and she walked right into Fulio's effusive embrace. His staff were lined up behind him, to pull out chairs, pour water, serve the crusty Italian bread for which the restaurant was famous.

As they were distributed among four tables for eight, Cordie was happy to find herself between Killian and Lew and across from Trilby Brown and Jack Eagan. John Crowder and the vice president and assistant vice president of public relations made up the rest of their table.

Killian table-hopped after everyone had ordered wine. The others were involved in a discussion about the best place to buy bagels in the city, giving Cordie the opportunity to catch up with Trilby. Her friend was a comfortably rounded brunette with a sunny disposition and a dream of owning her own millinery house if hats ever made a serious comeback.

She and Trilby had bonded instantly years ago at the wedding of a mutual friend who'd worked in the marketing department at Abbott Mills when Cordie had modeled for André McGinty. Her silence about Cordie's marriage to Killian had been partially responsible for Cordie's being hired by Abbott Mills. Cordie had confided her plot to Trilby, who'd endorsed it wholeheartedly.

"So, how's it going on the home front?" Trilby asked, leaning conspiratorially toward Cordie. "He seems very affectionate toward you. Everyone's talking about it."

Cordie nodded. "More wonderfully than I'd even dared dream. And he's happy about the baby. Which makes me very happy." Then she studied her friend, who seemed to have even more of a glow about her than usual. "And what's going on with you? Have you met someone?"

Trilby blushed. Trilby never blushed. She'd once tripped and fallen on her backside in front of Bloomford's with scores of people rushing by and laughing. She'd found it funny rather than embarrassing.

"Yes," Trilby admitted in a whisper, and put a finger to her lips to prevent Cordie from asking the obvious question.

Then she inclined her head to indicate the man next to her who leaned toward John Crowder as they talked animatedly.

Jack Eagan sat next to Trilby.

Cordie widened her eyes at Trilby, certain she'd mistaken the gesture. Jack was wonderful, but he was thirty years older than Trilby.

Trilby nodded to confirm that she had her eye on Jack.

"Okay," Cordie whispered. "But I want details at the first possible moment."

Killian returned, effectively putting an end to their conversation.

Fulio personally delivered to Cordie a wineglass filled with sparkling apple cider.

Steaming, aromatic minestrone was followed by spinach salad with a balsamic vinegar–Dijon mustard dressing. Oohs and aahs greeted the arrival of the prime rib and prawns, and conversation quieted to a low roar as everyone ate.

Killian nudged Cordie's hand as she moaned her

pleasure over a succulent shrimp. "Aren't you glad we didn't have to order ice cream for you?"

She put a hand to her heart in gustatory ecstasy. "I can't tell you how happy I am about that. This is beyond delicious."

"The baby's first words are probably going to be Hudson River Ice Cream."

"Well, he'll have to get his own flavor. The bar-ber-pole is all mine."

"'He'?" He speared a bite of vegetable. "Now you're thinking it's a boy?"

She made a face at him. "You've referred to the baby as 'he' so often I've been corrupted."

He checked to make sure their companions' attention was elsewhere before adding in a quiet, lasciv-ious tone, "Corrupted, huh? I'm glad to hear that."

She leaned toward him, her chin in her hand, and added quietly, "You did seem pleased with my plans for tonight."

His eyes stroked her. "I don't want to skip one thing on your schedule."

"I won't." Hers touched him back. "I promise."

KILLIAN WAS FOR PUTTING an end to dinner now and racing the bus back home. Or he and Cordie could simply leave everyone there and race home on their own. But these were the people who implemented his plans, improved them with their own ideas, pro-moted them and ultimately sold them. He owed them his success.

"Don't lose a fraction of the enthusiasm behind

that look in your eyes," he whispered, "until I get you where I want you."

"That's a promise, too," she said.

She was magnificent in the black dress molded to her body and to the baby. She'd combed her hair down, wove the swept-back ends into a braid so that the diamond combs could hold the weight of her hair. She was the picture of subtle glamour in evening makeup and her nearly bare shoulders. It was all he could do not to put his lips there in front of everyone.

He had to think about something else. Mercifully, Fulio chose that time to clear away plates, then served the tiramisu all his regulars raved about, Cordie particularly.

He poured a dessert wine to accompany the treat, then stopped at Killian's shoulder to ask if everything was to his satisfaction.

"It's perfection, Fulio," Killian replied. "You're unparalleled, my friend."

"Mmm," Cordie agreed, intoxicated with her favorite dessert. "If I'd met you first, Fulio, I'd be married to you."

"He was married before you were born," Killian pointed out.

"I'm not sure it would have mattered to her," Fulio teased, leaning a hand on the back of Killian's chair. He wore a spotless white apron over his white shirt and tie. "She hugged me in the drugstore yesterday." He smiled proudly.

"Obviously a hussy," Lew teased.

"And she and that young Mr. Girard had a lot to say to each other, too, so you'd better be on your guard, Mr. Abbott."

Fulio delivered that information on the crest of a jovial mood, completely unaware that he'd just dropped a grenade in the middle of their beautiful evening.

Killian's eyes swung to Cordie, their expression injured rather than angry.

She'd have willingly died by her own hand if someone hadn't already taken away her steak knife.

Everyone around the table probably knew the cause of her breakup with Killian and sat mutely by in great discomfort, waiting for Killian to reply.

Fulio, suddenly aware that he'd shared information he might have better kept to himself, stammered in an attempt to restore the happy mood.

"I…I mean…she…they only talked. I saw them through the window while I was sweeping. She was eating an ice cream and he…he…"

"Fulio." Killian stopped him in an even tone and with a smile Cordie was sure he'd manufactured. "It's all right. She knows everyone. If I got upset every time she spoke to another man, I'd have had to sell her into slavery long ago."

The tension dissolved and the guests laughed. Killian gave a credible performance of a man completely unaffected by Fulio's little joke. Only Cordie knew he was furious and probably planning to call that slaver tonight.

Or, worse, tell her to leave again.

The ride home on the bus was considerably different from the ride to town. Their companions were satiated and sleepy and barely conversed.

Killian hadn't looked at her since Fulio had mentioned Brian, though he kept an arm around her in the bus so that his anger wasn't apparent to anyone. But she felt the tension in him.

More than an hour passed before the house was quiet. Cordie, making sure their guests had everything they needed, waited in agony for Killian's return. He'd gone out to check the pavilion that Winfield had insisted looked unsteady, Elizabeth told her, so that the fall line could be hung first thing in the morning.

Elizabeth was clearly pleased that she knew Killian's whereabouts when Cordie didn't. Cordie was too worried to hate her.

The house was finally quiet when Killian came into the kitchen. He told Kezia, who was still fussing with trays for the following morning, to go home to bed.

She tried to protest, then took a second look at his face and did as he asked. She questioned Cordie with an arched eyebrow as she passed her.

Cordie folded her arms, refusing to act guilty about what had been a perfectly innocent encounter. She felt guilty, however, that she hadn't told him about it. "You want to talk?" she asked.

"Not here," he said, opening the door. "Outside."

She understood. He probably intended to shout.

And the house was quiet, but there was bound to be someone still up who'd happily listen to their raised voices and pass on what had been heard.

He headed off toward the pavilion he'd been checking on, clearly not caring whether or not she caught up. She hurried after him, running over an explanation in her mind.

He stopped in the middle of the shadowy tent and turned to face her. During the day, the pavilions were cool, sheltering places where the grass was more fragrant and the atmosphere festive.

At night, they were simply dark and a little scary. She ignored that and launched right into her explanation.

"As I told you, I went to the pharmacy, where I met Fulio, like he said, then I was going to hurry right home, but I was kind of enjoying the freedom for a little while and saw the ice-cream shop and thought I'd stop. I sat outside with a double-dip cone and Brian saw me and stopped. I know, I know, I could have walked away...."

"Yes," he said. "Presumably you hadn't just woken up this time."

She gave him an impatient look for that crack and continued a little aggressively. "But, yes, Brian and I *do* have a past. It's *friendship,* and I know something's going on with him. And anyway, he stopped to apologize for the other day."

Killian expelled a scornful half laugh.

"It's true!" she went on urgently. "He and his father had a parting of the ways and he bought the little general store down the beach.'' She waited to catch a glimpse of sympathy in Killian's behavior, but he just shook his head.

''Girard's a mean old man and he's well rid of him. But he's obviously keeping after you to get at me.''

''No. He stopped to apologize, and to give me a message for you.''

''What message?''

''He was the one who said not to buy the Florida Shops,'' she said. ''He said they were a losing proposition, that the daughter was really the brains behind the designs and lets her mother take the credit because she doesn't like the spotlight. And when the stores sell, she's going to work with André McGinty. It'd weaken your position and create an opening for his father to try a takeover or…something.''

He studied her doubtfully for a moment. ''We're too strong.''

''I'm only telling you what he told me. And there's no reason for him to lie—he's not part of the November Corporation anymore. I think you should listen to him.''

''Really.'' His quiet anger seemed to be heating up a little. ''Well, if you consider that message so important, why didn't you give it to me?''

His anger sparked hers, though she was completely aware she was at fault for much of this argument.

''Because I knew you'd misunderstand *just like you did before*.'' She added the last few words with particular emphasis. "And you'd react just like you're doing now."

He squared his shoulders. "I told you we'd shelved that."

She angled her chin. "Well, you're not behaving as though you have, are you?"

"Neither are you," he retorted, his voice rising a decibel. "Maybe this sympathy you have for him suggests feelings you just don't want to admit—at least not to me!"

"That's not true!" she shouted at him.

He turned to walk away from her and she caught his arm. "I'm not finished! You…!" Her heel stuck in the damp grass, effectively stopping her leg from following the forward thrust of her body as she went after him—or intended to. She caught the middle pole of the pavilion as she lost her balance. She went down with it. The canvas collapsed on top of her and Killian.

After the sound of poles clanking and the rush of falling canvas, she heard Killian's dry voice. "Good going, Cordelia."

THEY LAY on opposite edges of the bed, facing away from each other, the tension thick enough to collapse the mattress. Sawyer, coming home at just the right moment from a last-minute meeting about the fund-raiser for the Children with Cancer group, had hurried to their aid. Actually, hysterical laughter prevented him from helping very much, but he did manage to support one end of the canvas while Killian held it up so that Cordie could crawl out.

Sawyer wrapped his arms around her, still laughing while he asked her between fits if she was all right, leaving Killian to fend for himself.

He continued to laugh when she told him abruptly that she was fine and marched off to the house.

She'd have given a small fortune to be able to sleep anywhere but in Killian's room, but the house was bulging with guests, and short of being caught in the morning asleep on one of the sofas, there was no alternative.

She showered, changed into a pink cotton nightie and climbed into bed, thinking darkly that she'd been stupid to believe this would work. Stupid. Stupid. Apparently, the Brian debacle could not be shelved, no matter how many times Killian insisted he had. He'd misinterpreted what he'd seen—but he'd been shocked and disappointed, which had served his purpose for needing a reason to ask her to leave, and somehow in his anguish the details had become so entangled that he believed she'd been unfaithful. In all other aspects of his life, he was a fair and reasonable man, but that didn't seem to matter. He simply couldn't see straight when Brian was involved.

She felt a terrible sadness—worse than the last time—settle into the pit of her stomach, into her bones. She wasn't going to give up; it wasn't in her nature. Yet it was entirely possible she was fighting for a future that couldn't be.

She stared at the darkness beyond the window, unable to sleep. Killian had finally come up around midnight.

She clung to her side of the bed, pretending to be asleep while she heard him walk past her into the bathroom.

He was back in ten minutes, the fragrance of an herbal soap trailing after him. He climbed into bed, his movements angry but nowhere near her. She didn't feel a toe or a fingertip as he settled down and turned off the light.

She wept soundless tears, remembering how happy she'd been that morning, how much fun they'd all had at Fulio's until the restaurateur had mentioned Brian. Then she recalled that moment under the tree at lunchtime when Killian had encouraged her to tell him her plans for him tonight.

This wasn't at all what she'd promised.

KILLIAN LAY in the darkness, thinking righteously that no way could this be his fault. He'd grown up in a world of business and high finance where details were checked and double-checked and principal players were taught to protect themselves against deception and betrayal.

He'd done that his first go-around with Cordie, but this time he'd made every effort to ignore his suspicions and rely on the love in his heart. He'd decided to believe her about the hotel incident despite the overwhelming evidence, and look ahead rather than back.

He'd shared truths about himself even he hadn't known before. Then she'd met Brian, and if there had been nothing to the meeting, why *hadn't* she told him?

She'd claimed it was because she knew he'd react predictably—and he had. But wasn't that his right? How many times could a wife be found with the same man without a husband becoming suspicious? How many times had it happened to his father?

He lay still, disliking that the thought had occurred to him. He wasn't mistaking her for his mother. He was smarter than that. But he occasionally forgot to be smart where Cordie was concerned.

He never got angry in the boardroom because he knew that was deadly to making sound decisions that would affect his life and those of all his employees. But he had difficulty maintaining that emotional distance when his marriage and fatherhood were at stake.

That should be a good thing, he acknowledged, but as a man who generally knew more about business than he did about life, he could be wrong.

He closed his eyes and tried to empty his brain. Cordie's cologne clung to his pillow from last night. He refused to let an image of her naked take shape in his mind, but instead was treated to a picture of the way she'd looked tonight in the snug black dress with her small baby belly, her hair streaming down her back in a fat braid, the sides caught away from her face with the glittering combs.

He groaned quietly to himself and rubbed a hand

over his eyes to erase the image. That worked for an instant; then, absurdly, he remembered the moment Cordie had grabbed for him and the pavilion post at the same time and buried them in cotton duck. It surprised him that he was tempted to laugh. There was something seriously wrong with him.

He made himself relax with the reminder that he had to be up early tomorrow and that it was going to be a long day.

He was almost asleep a few moments later when Cordie made a violent turn in bed and thrust an arm out. "No!" she whimpered. "Where is she?"

He reached over to catch her hand as her voice grew more urgent. She was having a bad dream. But her hand was flailing in the darkness and he couldn't capture it until it slugged him on the chin.

"Cordie!" he whispered, unwilling to wake everyone in the rooms nearby. "Cordie, open your eyes!"

She struggled against him and began to cry. He put a hand over her mouth to silence the sound and pulled her to a sitting position, giving her a sound shake. "Cordie! Come on, Cordelia!"

Her eyes opened suddenly, their expression wide and frightened before she recovered from the nightmare. He turned on the bedside-table light.

"It was just a bad dream," he said, forgetting they were furious with each other as he brushed the tumbled hair out of her face. She was so pale and frightened. "It's all right. You're safe."

She looked at him in confusion, tears standing on her cheeks. "But where's…the baby?"

"The baby?"

"Abigail," she said.

A weird sense of déjà vu stole over him. He framed her face in his hands and asked, "My sister, Abigail?"

She shook her head, taking hold of his wrists. Her eyes held a fear he remembered seeing long ago in Chloe's eyes. "No, our baby. Our…our…Abigail…" Her voice trailed off as she finished the words, her eyes finally clearing of the remnants of the dream.

Her shoulders sagged and she pulled his hands down and placed one over her stomach. "Is she still there?" she asked anxiously. "Is there movement?"

He waited a moment, felt nothing but warm, supple flesh and the slight trembling that overtook her body.

"No," he said, pushing her back to her pillow and drawing up the blankets over her. "She's probably sleeping."

She stared at the ceiling, her eyes still frightened. "I dreamed she'd been…" She cast him an apologetic glance. "I'm sorry…I dreamed she'd been kidnapped." Then her face crumpled and she began to cry.

"Cordie, that was just a dream," he assured her. "She's still inside you, snug as a bug."

"Then what did that mean?"

"Dreams don't necessarily mean anything," he said practically.

Her dark eyes condemned him for such heresy.

"Okay, if it means anything, it's that you're tired and overstressed. But if you're afraid it means trouble, I'll take you to Dr. Rosenkrantz first thing in the morning and make sure."

She seemed to relax at that suggestion. Though she still looked troubled. "Maybe it means you'll try to take her from me. And I dreamed it's a her, not a him."

He reached over to turn off the light, then pulled her in to his shoulder and tucked the blanket in around her. "I'm not going to take him or her from you," he assured her, surprised to hear himself making that concession. In business dealings, he never compromised until he was sure he had what he wanted, what was best for Abbott Mills.

But this wasn't business. This was the mother of his baby frightened by a bad dream.

"You said you would," she reminded him.

"I told you I lied about that."

"You also told me you loved me."

"I do." Their argument badgered him in the darkness.

"Love believes what a lover says."

"It also tells the truth and doesn't leave anything out."

This was a strange disagreement to have in each other's arms, but he'd stopped trying to hold their relationship to any normally accepted standard.

She sighed, still snuggled against him. "Maybe we just don't know how to love each other."

That could be true. The feelings were certainly there, but reacting wisely to them and with them was another matter altogether.

"Yeah, well, we damn well better learn before the baby gets here," he said. "Go to sleep."

"I'm afraid the dream will come back," she admitted in a small voice.

"Dreams never come back in the same night."

"Who said?"

"It's fact. They might come back later, but never twice in one night. Like lightning never striking the same place twice." That was a bald-faced lie, but she apparently couldn't disprove it, though she seemed convinced dreams were significant.

"I'll make you pay if it does," she threatened.

"Mmm," he said, settling into his pillow. "Lucky for you I'm loaded."

Chapter Twelve

Cordie woke up feeling fine—at least physically. She was well rested after a good sleep—her nightmare excepted—and while in the shower, she experienced the flutter of movement again in her abdomen. Abigail was alive and well. It filled her with a satisfying sense of well-being. And hope.

Killian had been gone when she'd awakened, and Versace now lay on his pillow, fast asleep.

She heard Killian's voice and found him in the corridor, handing Lew a sheaf of papers. He was buttoning the cuffs of a dark blue shirt that made his eyes the color of this morning's sky. ''Sorry to put this on you,'' he was saying, ''but the doctor can fit us in in an hour and half, so we—''

''I'm fine,'' Cordie said from the doorway, touched that Killian had already called Dr. Rosenkrantz. But she couldn't disrupt this important weekend for a nightmare that had given her what amounted to simple dark-of-night fears.

When both men turned to her in surprise, she said,

"I'll phone Dr. Rosenkrantz and tell her every-thing's fine. There's no need to change plans."

"It might be a good idea to go anyway," Killian said, coming toward her. A little of the reserve he'd shown after Fulio's revelation was back again. She suddenly missed last night's closeness. "It'd get rid of any fears you have left over once and for all."

"No," she said firmly. "I'm fine this morning. I just had those willies you get when everything's dark and quiet and you come face-to-face with your worst fears. Besides, I have another appointment with her next week."

He studied her face as though analyzing whether she was telling him the truth. He would probably always do that now, she guessed—think twice about whatever she said.

"You're sure?" he finally asked.

She nodded. "I'm sure. You know I wouldn't take a chance."

"Okay." He turned to Lew. "You're off the hook after all."

Lew exaggerated a sense of relief. "Thank good-ness. Being you is harder than being me. I'm going to breakfast. You two want to join me?"

They went down the stairs together, Lew's pres-ence saving them from a discussion of what had hap-pened last night—both Killian's anger, then his un-derstanding and comforting response to her nightmare. She was happy to put off a discussion of last night, but wondered if she could survive the entire weekend without any real sense of where she stood.

After breakfast, the employees broke into small groups for creative sessions.

Cordie, feeling that being pregnant already had her actively engaged in being creative, wandered into the pavilion that Killian and Sawyer had put up again last night. The secretaries were making a display of the new fall line, the two young ones playfully sparring with mannequin arms while the older two fitted a very contemporary bustier on an armless mannequin.

"Isn't it incredible that this is back for evening?" Sharon asked Cordie. She worked for John Crowder, and was the epitome of grace and dignity. Elizabeth and her sparring partner, Tia from the secretarial pool, stopped guiltily and held their third arms in awkward embarrassment.

Cordie focused on Sharon. Terry from public relations stepped back to admire their work. "You have to admit they're sexy. There's a book out on the political implications of their popularity in the eighteenth and nineteenth centuries. At least today we can wear bustiers if we choose because they're not some man's idea of how we should look." She considered the blue denim one on the mannequin, then fingered the simple lines of the pin-striped gray bustier, leaning up artfully against the torso. "Can't you just see that over a plain white shirt?"

The three-armed young women stepped closer.

"That would be killer sexy," Elizabeth said. Every-one agreed.

Cordie found herself wondering if the adoring Elizabeth knew that Killian was called Killer by his brothers and close friends. She'd heard Lew use that nickname but never at the office.

"Good job, ladies," Cordie said, and moved on. She didn't suspect Killian of encouraging Elizabeth, but imagined the girl could go far on her own ro-mantic momentum.

"Listen to you," she grumbled as she set off across the grounds toward the beach. This session was scheduled to last two hours and she wouldn't be missed if she went to the water's edge for a little fresh air.

Sawyer was practicing his waterskiing jump this morning for the Children with Cancer fund-raiser. She might see him.

She enjoyed the brief walk through a clump of blueberry bushes, a grove of apple trees, then the gradual descent through beach grass and the leaning fences put up to prevent sand erosion. The air smelled of salt and diesel and the magic fragrance of early summer. Seagulls wheeled against a cloud-less blue sky.

She stopped briefly on a very shallow bank before the long stretch of beach and shaded her eyes for some sign of Sawyer. No one was out yet this morn-ing, but she did see something in the water about a hundred yards away.

She let out a horrified gasp when she was close

enough to identify Sawyer on water skis, and the small boat a short distance ahead of him, waiting for his signal. Eight barrels floated on the water, tied together just in front of a jump ramp. He intended to jump the barrels.

She wondered if Killian knew what Sawyer was doing. Then she realized that didn't matter. Killian couldn't have prevented Sawyer if he'd wanted to. He always said Sawyer thrived on the edge of destruction. Killian fought his demons by working all the time and resisting fun, and Sawyer dealt with his by taunting death.

She considered running back to the house, but there wasn't time. And she just wasn't the type who constantly carried a cell phone, unwilling to be out of touch. So all she could do was stand on the shore and watch.

She cheered herself with the thought that he'd been rehearsing this stunt all week. If he was still in one piece, he must have done it successfully several times.

She breathed a quiet prayer.

KILLIAN CONSIDERED the day off to a good start. All the employees seemed to be enjoying themselves, food was disappearing at a great rate—always a good sign, according to Kezia—and the creativity groups appeared animated and earnest.

He looked around for Cordie, wanting to make sure she was still feeling as well as she had felt at breakfast. Over bagels and fruit, wearing a soft pink shirt and shorts, her hair in a ponytail, she'd charmed a table filled with his sometimes sober staff. She told them stories about her parents, anecdotes about the years she'd spent modeling; offered prognostications on Abbott Mills's wonderful future.

And without warning, she talked about the impact plus-size fashions were making on the market. "It's something we should think about," she'd said. "Half of all adult Americans are overweight, but only nineteen percent of sales were from larger garments last year. That means half the market—that's plus-size women size fourteen and over—are buying only nineteen percent of the clothes. Somebody could make a fortune selling beautiful clothes to larger women. Why shouldn't it be us? Style has improved considerably in that area, but apparently not enough. Still some bad styling or poor fabric. If we're going to pick up more stores, we should look for something in the over-fourteen market. Or create our own."

She'd had them completely engaged, and when they had to be encouraged to leave breakfast to make their creative groups on time, there was a new quality to their looks of respect.

"That's a smart woman, Killian," Crowder told him. "Smart of you to find her." Then he grinned teasingly. "Or were you really attracted to her stellar beauty? Tell me the truth, now."

Killian remembered very clearly what it was about her that had attracted, then captured, him immediately. "No, it was her sunny disposition, her ability to see the cheerful side of everything," he said, then added in his own mind, her incandescence, which had brought light to his otherwise shadowy life.

By some miracle, she'd fallen in love with him, too, and he'd married her, sure he'd now be able to think ahead instead of back. And it had worked for about a month. Then one night, he'd checked his schedule for the following day and noticed with surprise that the day before had been the anniversary of Abby's kidnapping and it hadn't even occurred to him. Previously, he'd marked the day with memories of the pudgy baby and self-recriminations for having been absent from the house.

But that day, he and Cordie had gone to the movies, stopped at Fulio's afterward, made love in the boathouse because Sawyer had friends over.

He thought that over, seeing things a little more clearly since he'd been forced to look at things her way for a couple of weeks. That he'd forgotten that he'd failed his little sister had appalled and terrified him.

He felt the sun on his face now; absently heard the groups scattered around in the pavilions, talking; heard Kezia working with a whisk on something in the kitchen.

He remembered the eleven-year-old boy he'd been when police officers had picked him up at his friend's house and driven him home. He'd known something awful had happened, but no one would tell him anything until he got home and his father took him aside to explain that Abby had been abducted.

All he could think about was that every other night of his life since the day his mother had left, he'd sat at his bedroom window, or the window in what was now Cordie's turret room, and watched for her return. For a long time he'd held the conviction that it was impossible for him to love her so much and not have that love reciprocated. She was going to come back for him and Sawyer.

But the night Abby disappeared, he'd gone to a birthday party sleepover at a friend's house, privately deciding his vigil was over. He was growing up. He was beginning to understand what his father meant when he discussed business. He found it exciting, and even in his preadolescent mind he'd understood that he couldn't move ahead if he was weighted down by old beliefs that had proved themselves false. His mother wasn't coming back. So, he wasn't watching for her anymore.

Now he saw himself as the eleven-year-old sitting on the edge of the sofa while his father and the police officers asked if he recalled the men who'd worked in the house the previous week. They told him his father had said he had a very good memory, that he noticed everything and never forgot it.

Then he realized that if he'd been home, watching for his mother, he'd have seen or heard whoever had come into the house to take Abby. It was his fault she was gone.

He put a hand to his heart where a pain throbbed

with momentarily unbearable pressure. Years of self-
inflicted guilt were finally yanked out by clear, ma-
ture thought.

He'd been eleven years old! All the years since
he'd carried a guilt inflicted on him by the sorrowful
child he'd been and when Cordie had loved him so
much that he'd forgotten his pain, he'd blamed her
for his happiness. She'd lifted his misery and he'd
been so sure he'd have to atone for what he'd done
for a lifetime.

His crime had been a need to find his own happiness when he was the eldest, the one who had to
make sure his siblings were happy.

Even now there was a reluctance to let the guilt
go; it was all he had of Abigail. But he was about
to become a father, and he wanted to brighten the
world he lived in for his child, open it up to all the
good things out there.

He gasped as the pain stopped, rubbing where it
had been for so long.

"Mr. Killian." Winfield appeared beside him,
took his arm, and pushed him onto the garden bench.
"What's the matter? You're not having a heart attack, are you?"

"Ah…" He was so shaken by the sudden lightness of his person that it took a moment to answer.
"No, no. At least, not a bad attack."

Winfield blinked at him. "Is there a good one?"

Killian laughed. "Believe it or not, there is." He
had an uncontrollable urge to laugh out loud, to run,
to find Cordie and tell her that even if she did have

feelings for Brian now, he was going to love her so completely that there wouldn't be room in her soul for anyone but him. "Where's Cordie?"

He pointed north. "I saw her walking toward the orchard," he said. "About fifteen minutes ago."

"Thanks, Winfield." Killian took off at a run for the dusty lane that led through the blueberries and the trees to the beach. He felt like an Olympic competitor, moving faster than was humanly possible, finally free of all the old burdens of his life.

He had reached the beach and was so intent on finding a female figure in pink cotton with red hair that would catch the sun like a mirror that he didn't see the barrels in the ocean until he heard a motor rev and stopped to locate the sound.

Then he noticed the water-skier attached to the boat by the thin towline. He spotted the ramp they were headed for—and the long string of barrels lined up in front of it.

The expletive caught in his throat as he stared, involuntarily, having to watch what happened, even though a dark sense of dread was already taking over the lightness of being he'd enjoyed so briefly.

The motor roared, the boat led the skier away from the barrels for some distance, then made a wide, easy turn and hit the gas, heading the skier for the ramp.

Killian watched the action in grim fascination, as the boat skirted the ramp at the last moment. On the next pass, Sawyer's skis took the ramp. In perfect form, Sawyer soared over the barrels, and it looked as though he was going to make it until—unbelievably—a seagull squawked and swerved to avoid him. Instinctively, Sawyer ducked his head; his right ski dropped and caught the second-to-the-last barrel. He let go of the towline and fell against the last barrel as though he'd been body-slammed. Then his upper body slid into the water, his ski caught in the ropes that connected the barrels. From the fact that his brother didn't struggle, Killian guessed that Sawyer was unconscious.

That pain in his heart was back with a vengeance as he raced along the sand, thinking frantically that he'd never arrive in time, that there was little more than one airless minute until unconsciousness and six airless minutes until brain damage. It couldn't be, he thought in agony, that the only other person in the world who truly understood his dark places because he had the very same ones was being taken from him, too.

To his further horror, he watched the driver of the tow boat make a sharp turn to double back and, in his panic, stall the engine.

He ran harder. Then a figure swimming strongly toward the barrels from the other direction—some blessed bystander who'd seen the accident happen—snagged his attention. He glimpsed a flash of pink also swimming toward Sawyer. Cordie?

For an instant, he didn't know whether to be pleased that she was rushing to Sawyer's aid or upset that she was swimming too hard for a woman carrying a baby.

He stopped opposite the last barrel, pulled off his shoes and ran into the water.

The man, a strong swimmer, reached Sawyer as Killian was passing Cordie, telling her to go back. He kept swimming, his heart thundering in his ears as he watched the man pull Sawyer's face out of the water and hold it up. His ski still caught in the ropes, his leg at an awkward angle, Sawyer didn't move or even seem to breathe.

Then Killian felt as though he himself had stopped breathing when he finally reached them and saw that the man holding Sawyer's upper body against his shoulder to relieve the pressure on his trapped leg was Brian Girard.

A corner of his mind not occupied with the life-and-death struggle thought bleakly, Cordie and Brian—again. Brian's eyes met his. There was no dare in them this time, just the desperation of the moment.

"Watch it!" Killian cautioned him. "I'm going to climb up and free the ski. "The barrels'll move."

"Okay!" Brian replied. "I've got him."

Killian moved as carefully as possible, but the barrels bobbed and creaked and he heard Brian's grunt of effort. The ski was caught in the ropes lashing the barrels to the pontoons at the sides. He'd expected to find at least a compound fracture of Sawyer's lower leg or ankle, but it looked surprisingly sound. He was no doctor, but if the leg was broken, the fracture wasn't half as bad as he'd imagined.

"I'm going to free his foot!" he shouted at Brian. In the background he heard the sound of a motor struggling to start.

"Okay!"

"He'll be heavy!"

"He already is!"

Had Killian been less terrified, he might have smiled. He could only imagine the strength required to hold Sawyer's upper body over his head.

Killian freed Sawyer's foot from the wet boot, then did his best to ease Sawyer's leg into the water.

There was a cry of pain, a quiet "Ah!," and when Killian investigated, Sawyer and Brian had disappeared underwater. Only Cordie's bottom in her pink shorts was visible as she dived down after them like a cormorant. What the hell had happened?

He wanted to shout at God for standing idly by, then decided this wasn't the time to antagonize him. Killian didn't let himself think about why Brian had been there in the first place.

He went under, too, but had difficulty finding Cordie in the murky water.

They almost collided as she stroked one-handed and kicked upward, a man's shirt caught in her fist. She had Sawyer.

Killian helped her pull him up. She broke the surface, gasping for air. A big hand reached into the water to haul Sawyer into the tow boat, which had finally made it back.

"I'm going after Brian!" Cordie said, catching

her breath to go under again. But Killian grabbed her arm before she could dive.

"Take her aboard," he said to the boatman, then dived in search of Brian.

He swam off a few yards to where he'd met Cordie coming up. Since Sawyer and Brian had been side by side when they went down, Brian should be there, too.

Killian dived down, swinging his arms in wide arcs and encountering nothing. He went farther down in the turbid water. He swam in a circle around the area, going lower still. Then his hand connected with flesh and he grabbed. It was a man's arm.

Curling his arm around Brian's chest, he propelled himself upward, praying. Was Sawyer breathing? Were Cordie and the baby all right? What in the hell had Brian been doing there? And was he alive?

Killian surfaced a small distance from the boat and swam toward it. The boatman and Cordie both reached into the water to help pull Brian aboard. Killian noticed the dark bruise on Brian's head and wondered if Sawyer's body had hit him when he'd freed his foot. Or he might have been struck by one of the barrels.

The boatman started mouth-to-mouth instantly.

"How's Sawyer?" Killian asked Cordie, holding on to the side.

"He's breathing, but with difficulty," she said, wet and shivering. "He's in and out of consciousness. I think he's got some broken ribs. We called an ambulance." She helped Killian climb aboard.

"Are you all right?" he asked.

She nodded. "I'm fine."

Killian took the controls and aimed the boat for shore. Then he heard a cough and turned to see Brian drag in a noisy breath. Cordie put both hands to her mouth, then lowered them with a heartfelt "Thank God!"

Yes, he thought as he saw two ambulances come off the road and race down the beach as Cordie waved at them. Everyone alive. Hardly unscathed, but considering what could have happened, alive was good. He could worry later about what Brian was doing with Cordie.

By the time they reached the beach, Winfield, Daniel and Lew Weston were following the second ambulance on foot, a patrol car poking along behind them, wanting a way to pass.

The paramedics insisted on taking all of them in to Losthampton Hospital. When Killian assured them he was fine but that Cordie should see a doctor, Winfield and Lew pushed him toward the second ambulance.

"The trouble with this guy," Lew said to the paramedic, "is that he thinks he's in charge of the whole world. Maybe you could sedate him or something."

"I'm not hurt." Killian resisted their efforts to urge him into the ambulance.

"If you don't go," Cordie said, still shivering, "I won't go. And if this baby catches pneumonia, it's on your head."

That sounded like a woman who cared about him.

Killian heaved a sigh and followed her into the ambulance. Winfield, Daniel and Lew cheered her, promising to meet them at the hospital.

"Someone's got to stay and see to our guests!" he shouted out the doors.

"There's lots of food and we'll try to follow the afternoon schedule," Lew said, leaning around the closing doors. "But when we figured out it was you and Cordie in trouble, everyone was understandably worried. We may just have to pass on the Big Ideas session, *or do it tomorrow!*" The last phrase was added at full volume as the doors closed on him.

"You workaholic types," the paramedic said to him as he helped Cordie lie back on a gurney. He was a big dark-haired man about Killian's age, with a wide smile despite his criticism. "Don't know enough to stop long enough to take care of yourselves. Lie down on that bunk." He indicated the one on the opposite side. "And I don't want any trouble out of you."

Killian cooperated. This was probably not the time to tell him that his family had built the hospital.

"Will you just make sure that she's all right?" he asked, pointing to Cordie. "She's four and a half months pregnant and she swam pretty hard, dragged my brother to the surface…"

"Actually, I thought I'd just find something on the radio until we got to the hospital." The paramedic spoke as he studied the monitors to which he'd already hooked up Cordie. "You know, kick back, do nothing, let the doctors handle it when we arrive.''

"Smart guy.''

"No. Just capable. Take it easy, Mr. Abbott. Your lady's vital signs are very good. Heart's beating a little fast, but she just rescued your brother, right?''

"If he'd had his way,'' Cordie teased, "I'd have gone back to shore like he told me to do when he swam past me. But I had a sneaking suspicion he might need me. So I ignored him.''

Killian made a face at her around the paramedic's leg. "I didn't want you to get hurt. But I did need you, so thank you for ignoring me. I'm sure that won't be the last time you do it.''

The paramedic laughed. "You two are a riot. Now, both of you be quiet so I can do my thing here.''

"But he—'' Cordie began.

"Shh!''

The same thing happened at the hospital. At the office, Killian's very presence was respected and everyone stopped to hear what he had to say. Here, they not only ignored him, they asked him to be quiet.

"He's the man whose father built this hospital,'' the nurse said under her breath to the E.R. doctor looking over Cordie. Sawyer and Brian had been taken into other rooms. Killian, the paramedic had determined, *was* fine.

The doctor looked into Cordie's eyes with a light. "You could have made the lounge a little bigger,'' he said to Killian, then straightened to grin. "Otherwise, it's a great place. Thank you. And your wife and baby seem to be very healthy, but I'd like an OB-GYN to examine her to be sure."

"I agree."

"How are Sawyer and Brian?" Cordie asked.

"Not sure yet," Killian replied. "Winfield's trying to find out. Daniel and Lew are in the waiting room."

"You built us a beautiful cafeteria," the doctor said, pointing toward the long hallway visible beyond the draperies. "You and your friends should go there, have a cup of coffee, and when Dr. Carmelo is here—that's the obstetrician—I'll call you. You relax, Mrs. Abbott. Dr. Carmelo's on her way."

"I'll be right back," Killian promised Cordie.

"I'm good." She closed her eyes. "You go have a cup of coffee with the guys, I'll wait here."

He studied her, pale and slender on the table except for the little mound of her pregnancy, and remembered how quickly she'd headed for Sawyer, how stubbornly she'd ignored Killian's directive to go back to shore, how grateful he was that she had when Sawyer and Brian disappeared underwater.

He suddenly remembered that Brian had been swimming from a completely different direction than she had. Had they not been together after all? Or had they been on their way to a meeting, but the accident had prevented it?

This was not the time to ask.

Instead, he took her hand and kissed it.

"Thanks," he said, "for coming to Sawyer's rescue. But…what happened out there? One minute Brian had Sawyer, and the next they were both under."

"The pontoon bounced," she said, "and slapped against the side of Brian's head. He was focused on holding on to Sawyer when you freed his foot and didn't see it coming. Thank God he was there!"

She sounded surprised that he had been. Or was she protecting Killian from some truth about Brian as she had when they'd talked in town? He'd have to worry about that later, too.

"Okay." He kissed her hand again. "Doze for a few minutes. I'll be right back."

Killian told Daniel and Lew how to find the cafeteria, then prepared to go in search of Winfield, who was attempting to learn Sawyer's condition.

As he passed a hallway, he saw Campbell running toward the door from the parking lot. He was wearing a suit and slowed his rapid pace when he spotted Killian going toward him.

"How is he? What happened?" he demanded. "Kezia told me there was an accident with the stunt, but she didn't have any details."

"He's still in X ray." Killian put a hand on his shoulder in an effort to slow him down. "Take a breath. He's going to be all right." He explained what had happened. "His leg didn't look broken, but he slammed against the barrels so hard I'm fairly sure he cracked some ribs."

Campbell accepted that with a hand to his heart

and a sigh of relief. "How's Cordie? Is the baby okay?"

"The E.R. doc seems to think so, but he wants an obstetrician to examine her, so we're just waiting for her to get here. Want a cup of coffee?"

Campbell pulled at his tie and unbuttoned the collar of his dress shirt. He expelled a breath. "Yeah. I guess. Geez, I leave you guys for two days and I come home to find everybody in the hospital! Why are you wearing those doctor clothes?"

Killian glanced down at the light blue scrubs, then up at his brother. "Deep water, wet clothes, remember? All of us are drenched."

"Oh, yeah. Incidentally…" He stopped him as they would have moved on toward the cafeteria. "What was Brian Girard doing there?"

Killian stepped out in faith and told him what he chose to believe. "I have no idea," he said. "He was already in the water and swimming toward Sawyer when I noticed him. He may even have saved Sawyer's life. He kept his face out of the water until I could release Sawyer's foot."

Campbell was frowning, and Killian could guess what he was thinking. "If Cordie was meeting him," he finally said quietly, "I'm convinced that she was doing it to tell him she loves me."

"She does, you know," Campbell said.

"Yeah. Come on."

Winfield had already joined Daniel and Lew by the time Killian and Campbell arrived at the cafeteria.

"Still in X ray," Winfield said, sipping a cup of coffee. "But he had the technician's assistant giggling, so he's probably not feeling too badly. The doctor will come and get us when he's finished."

Campbell and Killian went to a small table set up with a coffeepot and cups, poured their coffees, then returned to the table.

"You're home a day early," Winfield said to Campbell. "Without benefit of helicopter."

"You missed it." Campbell got up again to go for cream. "I did arrive by helicopter, but at the airport, and one of Killian's people picked me up since Daniel wasn't there. A pretty little brunette named Elizabeth."

"She has a thing for Killian," Lew said. "It'd be nice if you could take the heat off him."

"Happy to."

Killian wondered suddenly if Campbell had gotten the job, but didn't want to ask him in front of everyone. And he wasn't sure he really wanted to know, anyway.

A nurse appeared in the cafeteria doorway. "Mr. Killian Abbott?" she called.

Killian stood.

"Dr. Carmelo's arrived," she said. "Your wife sent me to get you."

Killian stood and pushed his chair in. "If you hear anything about Sawyer," he said to Campbell, "would you come and tell me?"

"Sure. Go."

Dr. Carmelo was a very pretty middle-aged

woman with a quiet nature that inspired confidence and calm. She was rubbing some gelatinous stuff on Cordie's belly when Killian walked into the room. He smiled at her, but Cordie could see the turbulence in his eyes.

"Is Sawyer okay?" she asked anxiously, reaching for his hand.

"I think so," he replied, taking hers and coming to the bed. "He's still in X ray."

The doctor looked up to smile at him. "Hello, Mr. Abbott. Pull that stool over. I'm about to show movies. In the city, I have a technician to do this for me, but in little Losthampton, I get to do it myself. I love that."

Killian caught the stool with his foot and drew it toward the bed.

Cordie was worried about his expression. She knew he was wondering what Brian had been doing on the beach. All his old suspicions had probably risen to the fore but he was ignoring them because he had more important things to worry about—his brother's safety, the baby.

The baby. She hadn't felt movement since she'd come out of the water. Though she'd assured Killian that she was fine, she'd held her breath for a long time when she'd gone down for Sawyer. And it was so easy to believe that this perfect life with Killian and their baby had been just a tease and she couldn't have it after all.

She gripped his hand, her fears threatening to take

over as the doctor fiddled with buttons on the ultrasound.

Killian gazed into her anxious face and put a hand to her still-damp hair piled under a cap. "Are you worried?" he asked gently.

Her lips trembled. "I was just thinking," she replied, her voice frail, "that we averted tragedy with Sawyer and Brian. I was wondering…if we can get lucky enough to do it again with the baby."

"Of course we can," he said firmly. "You changed my luck."

She closed her eyes and a tear trickled down. "I haven't felt anything since I came out of the water."

"He's probably just resting after the swim."

She looked up at the doctor, who was concentrating on her work. "There!" the doctor said, pointing to the screen.

Killian leaned forward. Cordie raised her head to see. Finding anything discernible in the swirled pattern on the screen was hard.

Then the doctor touched a spot with her finger. "See that? A head. A hand."

Cordie heard herself squeal.

The doctor pointed to a pulsing object. "A beating heart," she said with a smile for Cordie.

Cordie felt that her own stalled. Relief washed over her like warm bathtub water. She cried and laughed at the same time. "Killian!" she exclaimed, tears streaming down her face. "A beating heart!"

"Whoa," the doctor said.

"What?" Killian demanded. Cordie propped up on an elbow. "What's wrong?"

"Nothing's...wrong," she said distractedly as she fiddled with buttons on the machine. "Let's just turn up the sound." Suddenly, there was a weird whoosh, then the sound of a heartbeat.

She moved the device on Cordie's belly to the right and there was another sound, slightly different from the other.

"What's that?" Killian asked.

The doctor smiled. "Another heartbeat."

Cordie turned to Killian, afraid to believe that not only had they been that lucky but twice that lucky. And a corner of her mind not occupied with the baby—babies—wondered if he still wanted a life with her.

Or just the babies. He was watching the screen in complete absorption.

Cordie looked at the monitor, then at the doctor. "But I've heard that the sound can bounce around. That you can get the same heartbeat twice."

The doctor nodded. "That's true. But the heartbeats are different. Listen." She moved the device again to the original steady thrum, then to the other—a slightly different rhythm.

Cordie heard both in astonished delight. "But where's the second baby on the screen?"

"Probably behind his or her brother." She pointed to the very subtlest suggestion of genitalia on the baby in the foreground.

"Brother," Cordie breathed to Killian. "Two

babies,'' she said, wanting him to be as thrilled as she was, wanting him to want her as much as he wanted the baby.

He held her tightly and she felt the emotion in him. Relief, she supposed, that the babies were fine. Astonishment like her own that there were two healthy babies.

''And they're both all right?'' he asked the doctor, apparently needing to hear the blessings confirmed.

''We've got two strong little heartbeats. If you take good care of their mother, there's no reason they won't be born healthy and ready to change your lives forever.''

He held Cordie to him another moment. ''Thank God,'' he said, his voice thick and soft. ''And Cordie's okay?''

''Cordie is perfect. I'll make two copies of this picture for your baby books.'' She hit another button. ''I guess you'll have to tell the second baby it was hiding behind its brother.''

The doctor made two prints, wiped the gel stuff off Cordie's belly, then helped her sit up.

''That does it,'' she said. ''You can get dressed.'' Then she grinned. ''Or, I guess you can't. You have to wear our scrubs home.'' She handed the pictures to Cordie. ''My only advice is what you're probably already been doing. Eat well, get some exercise, do your best to stay mellow and be happy, and in October, you're going to deliver two beautiful, healthy babies.'' She shook Cordie's hand, then Killian's. ''Congratulations,'' she said.

Killian and Cordie stared at each other, then he burst into laughter and wrapped his arms around her. "Twins! We're having twins!"

She couldn't stand it another minute. She opened her mouth to ask him if he was wondering what Brian was doing at the beach. But she didn't know why he'd been there, either, so she wouldn't even be able to offer an excuse for Brian's presence. And Killian was probably tired of listening to excuses, anyway.

But habit died hard, and she had to try. "I was just taking a walk," she said, reaching for the scrubs the nurse had left for her, "when I saw what Sawyer was about to do, then witnessed the accident. I started swimming toward him…"

He nodded, waiting for her to continue. She pulled on the pale blue pants and top, wondering how she could make him understand that she loved him more than anything, that having a life with him and their babies was all she wanted.

The scrubs on, she yanked off the cap and tried to comb through her hair with her fingers.

"I should have stayed to help at the house," she said, agitated, angry, aware that her attempt to explain was taking a detour. "But I couldn't stop thinking about our fight last night, the nightmare, and I—" Her ring caught in her tangled hair and he came to help her extricate her fingers.

"Go on," he said.

"Well, I have no idea where I stand," she said, her voice high and much too loud. "You're mad at me one minute, holding and comforting me the next. And I adore you, but you're making me crazy!''

She delivered that last line as a nurse leaned into the doorway and said that Sawyer's doctor wanted to talk to him.

Cordie subsided, resolved that this wasn't the time to have this out. Sawyer was more important at the moment.

KILLIAN, confused and exasperated, took Cordie's hand and followed the nurse to Sawyer's room. They encountered Campbell, Winfield and Daniel along the way. Killian had to shift emotional gears from angst over his marriage to grave concern about his brother.

Sawyer sat up on the side of the bed while the doctor secured a bandage wrapped around him from under his pecs to just below his rib cage. He winced, then made a slow rumbling sound in his throat.

''Want to change your mind about the pain medication?'' the doctor asked.

''I think so,'' Sawyer said in a breathy voice. ''Yeah. Hi, guys.''

''Hi,'' Killian replied, wanting to tell him what he thought of this latest in a long line of death-defying—or death-inviting—stunts. But Sawyer would merely argue that it was for charity and brought in a lot of money. Only his family understood that he was driven to challenge his longevity— they just didn't understand precisely why.

And he didn't need another unhappy issue, anyway.

Sawyer smiled at Cordie. "Hey, sis. Glad to see you're okay." He sobered. "How's the baby?"

She didn't seem able to hold back a grin, despite her annoyance over their relationship, "Plural, thank you." Then she grinned at Killian.

Sawyer clearly didn't get that. "Plural," he repeated. Frowning at Killian, then at the grin he, too, couldn't contain, said in disbelief, "No!"

"Yes," Killian confirmed.

"Twins?" Campbell demanded.

"Yeah."

Campbell wrapped his arms around Cordie. "That's great! Do we know what gender?"

"One boy," she said, hugging him back. "The other one's hiding."

"Wow!" Sawyer stepped off the table, then winced and put a hand to his bandage. The doctor steadied him.

"He has to lie low for a few days," the doctor said, reaching for a bottle of pills. The nurse brought him a glass of water. He handed a pill and the glass to Sawyer.

"It's painful for him to breathe, to swallow, to move," the doctor warned. "He's been extremely lucky that his lungs weren't punctured. And he's pulled the muscle on that leg, but nothing's broken. His guardian angel was on duty today."

"I think his guardian angel quit some time ago,"

Killian said. "God himself is handling his case. That's why Sawyer's still here."

Sawyer winced as he swallowed the pill. The doctor handed him the bottle. "Twice a day as long as you're feeling uncomfortable."

"Aren't you home early?" Sawyer asked Campbell, his voice gravelly with pain.

Campbell nodded. "Got finished early."

Killian hoped Campbell would explain further, but he didn't.

"He can go," the doctor said, taking Sawyer's arm to help him to his feet. Killian reached for the other arm. "He'll have to wear these scrubs home. His clothes are drenched." Then he noticed Killian also wearing scrubs and grinned. "But then, you know all about being drenched, too, don't you?"

"That I do."

Sawyer held tightly to Killian's arm as Campbell took over for the doctor on his other side. "Do I remember…Brian Girard helping me in the water?" he asked Killian.

Killian nodded, recounting how Brian had kept Sawyer's face out of the water and supported his upper body. "When I untangled your ski, the pontoons bobbed and hit him in the head. He's next door."

"Brian Girard," Sawyer repeated.

"Yes."

"Why would he save me? He hates us."

"I don't hate you." Brian's voice came from the doorway of the hospital room.

Killian looked up to see Brian, also in scrubs, with a plastic bag that probably contained his wet clothes dangling from his hand. He wore his shoes without socks, just as Sawyer, Killian and Cordie did.

And he sported a large purple bruise on the side of his otherwise pale face. "How are you?" he asked Sawyer.

Sawyer, agape for a moment, finally replied, "Just a few broken ribs. Thanks to you, I understand."

Brian shrugged. "Cordie was heading for you. I thought I'd better reach you first before she hurt herself trying to get you out of the water." He noticed Cordie and smiled at her. "Are you and the baby all right?"

"We're fine," she said, going to give him a quick hug. "We have twins."

He laughed lightly. "You're kidding!" Then he turned to Killian. "You always were an over-achiever."

"Where were you coming from, anyway?" Cordie asked Brian. "When I was swimming for Sawyer, I saw you heading toward us from the beach."

"I was testing the seaworthiness of the rental boats I bought along with the general store," he replied. "A little canoe was practically sinking under me when I saw Sawyer go flying through the air."

So that explained it. Killian was almost hysterical with relief.

There was silence for the space of a heartbeat, then Sawyer said, "Thank you, Brian."

Brian nodded, a strangely melancholy look in his

eyes. Killian would have thought that a happy ending in which he'd played such an important part would have warranted more cheer. Particularly since Brian had just said he *didn't* hate them. "You're welcome." The he turned to Killian, the adult version of the kid he'd scrapped with so much of his life. Inexplicably, there was a sudden grace about him Killian didn't understand. "Thank you. The paramedic told me you dived for me and brought me up."

"I did. Cordie again. She was going to do it herself."

He laughed, a completely uncomplicated laugh— an understanding of Cordie's sometimes heroic determination. Something for the first time ever that they could share.

"And while I'm explaining," he said, "I should tell you that when you found me in Cordie's room in Paris, I was giving her my second key. I'd gotten it for a girl who was making eyes at me during the show that afternoon, but we never did get together. Anyway..." He hunched a shoulder apologetically. "When you saw me there and became all bluster and accusation, I got a charge out of letting you believe I was after Cordie. And that day in the parking lot at Fulio's was simple meanness. You had her back, and though all she'd ever been to me was a friend, I resented that again you had more than I'd ever have—friends and family who loved you."

Then the mood changed swiftly and that sadness came over him again. "Goodbye," he said. "Congratulations on the babies.'' He turned and began to walk away.

A doctor beyond the curtain caught his arm. ''Mr. Girard, you really should have someone keep an eye on you overnight.''

''I'll be fine, Doctor. Thank you.''

''Ah…'' Killian cleared his throat. He could deal with being wrong, but hated being wrong *and* stupid. ''How are you getting home, Brian?''

''Cab,'' Brian replied. ''Please don't worry about me or feel unduly grateful. Anybody would have done the same thing. I just happened to be there. And you did the same for me, so we're even. Quits.''

''Why don't I take you home to your father's?'' Killian asked.

''He's in the city.''

''Certainly his staff can keep an eye on you tonight.''

Brian grinned grimly. ''I don't think so. But, thanks.''

Killian couldn't believe the thought that came to mind. Then he caught Cordie's eyes and saw her silent plea to do something. After all he'd put her through, he owed her that.

He turned to Sawyer, who was pretty good at reading his mind and encountered a raised eyebrow, followed by a curious twitching of his lips. Campbell, who could often intuit what was on Killian's mind, stared at him with a mixture of incredulity and support.

"Brian!" Killian shouted as Brian started down the corridor. He'd saved Sawyer's life and he'd been unfairly judged. There had to be a way to make a friend of him. "Come home with us. The house is crowded with business guests for the weekend, but there's room for you if Sawyer will share the boathouse. Campbell will keep an eye on the two of you tonight."

The melancholy in Brian's eyes liquefied into some deep emotion out of all proportion to the simple suggestion, even considering their previous animosity.

Brian stared at Killian for a long moment, glanced at his brothers, then swallowed hard. With an indrawn breath, he said unsteadily, "Thanks, but I was looking over the general store and left it unlocked. I had the boat keys in my pocket—"

He couldn't stop talking.

"But I don't seem to have them anymore. I've got to go back and make sure everything's…secure."

"Winfield will drive you back," Killian said, "then take you to our place."

"I—"

"Brian!" A booming voice sounded from behind him. Brian apparently recognized it instantly and so did Killian. It was Corbin Girard. Brian closed his eyes for a moment before turning to his father.

"Hello, Dad," he said.

Corbin was of medium height and stature, but with a meanness that should have required a much larger host. He had a reputation for merciless dealings in every phase of his life.

"You don't appear to be at death's door to me," he said, looking his son up and down with an almost disappointed expression. "Abbott's housekeeper called to tell me they took you off in an ambulance."

"Yes."

"Are you going to live?"

"Sorry. Yes, I am."

Corbin made a scornful sound and jutted his chin into the room, where Killian, Sawyer and Campbell stood together. "With them?"

"Dad…" Brian cautioned quietly.

With them? That seemed such an odd question to Killian he felt compelled to explain why they were together if Brian was going to take heat for it. "Brian saved Sawyer's life. We were just thanking him."

The old man made that scornful sound again. "You're never going to learn, are you?" he asked Brian. "It'll never work. They're better than everybody. You'll never belong."

And that was even more odd. Killian turned to Brian for some clue to what the old man was talking about, but Brian was trying to pull his father with him toward the door.

The old man punched him hard in the shoulder.

"Hey!" The doctor, who'd been standing by in silence, intervened.

"This man has a mild concussion," he said, getting between Corbin and Brian.

"This man," Corbin said with an angry glance at his son, "was born with a mild concussion. You think they're going to treat you better than I did?"

"Dad..." Brian appeared to be in misery.

Killian felt that he was in the twilight zone.

"You think they're going to take you into their hearts and home because their cheating mother was your mother, too?"

Killian heard those words like a cymbal crash, then the room fell deadly quiet. Killian struggled to put meaning to the words, but his brain wasn't working. Sawyer inhaled sharply and Killian held on to him a little more tightly.

"What?" he heard himself ask.

Corbin came to stand within two inches of his face. "You think that chauffeur was the first man your mother fooled around with? I came first, or maybe second or third, but I had a paragon of a wife and an empire to run and I couldn't just take off with her to cruise the seas and ride camels and fulfill all her childish fantasies. So I told her she'd have to tell your father the baby was his."

Killian was hearing him, but he wasn't sure he was absorbing the facts. The sound seemed to be flying by him like the scenery when he opened up the Jag's engine.

The old man was taking great delight in sharing his shocking message. "What I didn't know was they hadn't slept together in six months, and that untruth just wouldn't fly. So she left with the chauffeur to have the baby in England. She'd apparently explained the baby to him, because when she died giving birth, he called to tell me. Unfortunately, I was in Japan doing business and he spoke to my wife. When I came back, my wife had already brought Brian home. She insisted we raise him and tell everyone he was adopted, that it was my duty.''

Killian pushed the old man away from him and turned to Brian, wondering how he'd lived his entire life knowing all that and having to deal with his father's resentment.

''I *didn't* know,'' Brian replied, reading his mind. ''I couldn't imagine why he agreed to adopt me when it was clear he had no use for me. Then, when you won the Businessman of the Year award over me, he told me the truth—just to hurt me for not even having been in contention. And somehow that made it worse.'' He folded his arms tightly, his eyes turbulent and pained. ''He really was my father, and he still hated me because I was the indiscretion he had to pay for day after day for the rest of his life. All he'd done was fool around with his neighbor's wife—usually a safe bet for a man like him even if there was a pregnancy. Unless he was married to a woman with scruples who thought he should raise the child he sired.''

Tears welled in his eyes and he swiped them away with the heel of his hand. ''I used to watch the three of you at school,'' he said, looking from Killian to Sawyer to Campbell, ''and be so jealous that you had one another. But I used to hate you, Killian, for always being better than me, for proving my father's attitude about me. Then, when we got older, I gave you a run for your money in sports. You fought hard, but you were always fair. My father said I couldn't be friends with you, because the Abbotts were the enemy.

"I'd figured out he was wrong by the time I was a teenager, but our combative relationship was established and I didn't want you to think I was less tough than you were by suggesting friendship.

"We grew up and started fighting each other financially, and then my father told me the truth and I couldn't let you buy the Florida Shops when I knew the inside story, so I told Cordie to make sure you knew."

Killian turned to Corbin. "Is that why you threw him out?"

"I threw him out," the old man replied, "because he's no damn good to me. He's soft. He doesn't have the guts for business."

Brian listened to that abuse and shrugged helplessly. "I finally understood why I'd always felt a connection to all of you. We share blood." He made that gesture again and Killian completely understood its heartfelt, silent shout that the child of a heartless woman pays for her thoughtlessness his entire life. "It wasn't very good blood, I guess, but we've got it in common."

Killian freed Sawyer's arm and took a step forward.

CORBIN, Cordie noticed, took a step back.

She recognized Killian's warrior stance. "Killer"

had overtaken his usually courteous self. She saw Sawyer and Campbell exchange a look.

"Don't underestimate Stewart blood because of Susannah," Killian said. "Because it ran through a young farmer at the Alamo. A dance-hall girl who married a miner who made it big in the gold rush and built a town. Wildcatters in Midland, Texas, who doubled and tripled their inheritance from the miner and donated a college to that town. A doctor who opened a free clinic on the Mexican border. Our mother's brother died in Vietnam. She had no pride in the blood in her veins, but we do, and if you're going to be part of this family, you'll have to change your attitude."

A righteous head of steam clearly built up, Killian faced down Corbin Girard and felt Sawyer and Campbell lined up beside him, Sawyer with a pale face and a hand at his ribs.

"You came here to hurt Brian, not out of concern for him. You want to play takeover with me I'm ready for you. But I'm about to make a move you can't beat. I'm taking Brian."

He turned to Brian, who watched in astonishment, and asked, "You want in with us? We fight all the time, make one another nuts, but we appreciate one another's value, and we're so damn productive it's disgusting."

Brian was speechless for a moment. Then he asked, "You mean…?"

"Brotherhood," Sawyer simplified for him.

"How old are you?" Campbell wanted to know.

Brian's eyes lost focus, as he was momentarily distracted by the apparent non sequitur. "Thirty-two."

Campbell groaned. "Great. Another one older than I am. Well, hell. What's one more. Are you in?"

Brian suddenly grinned from ear to ear. "Yeah," he said, taking sides with the Abbotts as though someone had drawn a line on the hospital-room floor. "I'm in."

Cordie didn't care what Killian had decided about letting her stay, because she was in, too.

Chapter Thirteen

In his element ordering his troops, Killian ignored
Corbin's sputtering and told Campbell to take Brian
to the general store to secure it, then drive him back
to the house.

Brian tried to protest that no one had to watch
him, that he appreciated their kindness, but he had
a more-than-comfortable place to stay.

Campbell suggested he save his breath. "Don't
get in his way when he's like this. You'll only get
trampled. Come on."

With Daniel at the wheel, Killian put Sawyer in
the limo with Lew, pushed Cordie in behind them
and climbed in after her.

"Wow," Lew said wryly. "Who saw that coming?"

Everyone was still too startled to reply.

"Mr. Abbott," Daniel said, his eyes in the mirror
directed at Killian.

"Yes?" Killian glanced up, a little shaken himself
now that the battle was over.

"It's an honor to work for you, sir. Lots of people

in your world are great because of what they have. But you're great because of what you are.''

Lew nodded and smiled at Killian across the facing seats. ''I second that,'' he said.

Winfield folded his arms. ''I can also agree with that, but I don't know how I can be expected to protect you when you travel to foreign countries, perform death-defying stunts every time I turn around and invite all and sundry to come and stay with us. If this continues, I'll need a bigger staff.''

The laughter that resulted was a relief to everyone but Sawyer, who winced in pain as he began to join in.

At the house they were surrounded by Abbott Mills employees, who rushed to the limousine to help Sawyer into the house and inquire solicitously about the others involved in Sawyer's adventure.

''Mrs. Abbott needs a rest,'' Killian said as everyone clustered around him. ''She's fine,'' he added when they expressed concern, ''but we just found out she's carrying twins.''

There were cheers and applause.

''Thank you! Dinner's inside tonight.'' He glanced at his watch. ''In about an hour. Why don't you all explore the grounds, have a rest, whatever you prefer to do and we'll reconvene in the great room for a seafood buffet.''

More cheers and applause and they all dispersed. Killian said to Cordie, ''I know you're exhausted, but I'd like to talk to you for a few minutes.''

Her heart thrummed uncomfortably, seemed to be

beating in her throat. Her voice came out raspy and broken. ''Sure,'' she said.

KILLIAN DREW Cordie with him to his bedroom and wondered how on earth he could convince her to stay with him once the babies were born. He'd just been proved a complete idiot, and though he was more remorseful than he could ever convey, he couldn't imagine she would forgive him. Despite all his brilliant business strategies of the past, the only thing he could think of at the moment was throwing himself on her mercy and groveling.

He sat her down on the edge of his bed. Versace got up from Cordie's pillow with a large yawn, turned in a circle, then settled down again, shielding his face with a paw. Killian thought absently that he was gradually morphing into a reasonable pet. Apparently, he wasn't the only one learning to sheathe his claws and trust the world he lived in.

''Cordie,'' Killian began, his voice tight as he realized the gravity of his situation and all he stood to lose. He paced the carpet in front of her. ''I'm so sorry that I jumped to conclusions about you and Brian, and that I didn't listen when you attempted to explain.''

''Killian…''

He kept talking. ''My childhood was so full of murky places that when you walked into my life, I couldn't believe that kind of happiness could happen to me.''

''Killy, I…''

"So I tried to push you away rather than wait for the day our life together fell apart on me."

"Killian!" she shouted, and got to her feet. Her eyes were dark with feeling, her mouth determined. He had to stop her before she announced that she was leaving.

"Tell me you'll stay," he pleaded, taking her hands. "Tell me you can forget that I—"

Before he could finish, she yanked a hand from his, caught the neck of the scrubs he wore and pulled him down until they were mouth to mouth. He experienced a moment of stunned disbelief when he felt the tip of her tongue against his, but got over it sufficiently to respond.

"You're forgiven," she said, her eyes gentling, her lips smiling. "If it makes you feel any better, I am a liar. I had Trilby help me get the job so we'd be in contact again because I *knew* you'd want your baby when you found out about it, and that would give me time to win you back. When I had my physical, I told the doctor it was all right to put the pregnancy in his report. I wanted you to find out."

To know she'd plotted this warmed him. He looped his arms around her.

"Really," he said, the sun coming out for him, though dusk had fallen. "That's very clever of you. So I don't have to lock you in the turret room after all to make you stay?"

She raised her face to kiss him again. "Not unless you lock yourself in with me."

He held her to him, a sort of reverence in his embrace that would enrich her for a lifetime.

"Do you remember the plans you had for me last night," he asked, "before you dumped a pavilion on me?"

"Yes, I do," she whispered.

"Well...I'd like to see some action on that project."

"But the house is full of people."

"I don't care. My heart is full of you."

Epilogue

Sawyer wandered up from the boathouse just before 7:00 a.m. Campbell and Brian were still sound asleep, but pain had prevented him from sleeping very well. His ribs felt as though he'd swallowed someone who was banging to get out. Someone with a horned helmet and golf shoes.

There was no sign of stirring from the house. The party had gone on late last night and they were probably all sleeping in. He knew Killian had asked everyone to stay an extra day because Crowder claimed to have researched Cordie's idea about plus-size clothing and had made some potentially important discoveries.

Sawyer went around to the side porch, intending to go in through the library—and was surprised to see the curvaceous back of a young woman in white pants and a white sweater. She was peering into the French doors.

"Can I help you?" he asked.

The woman turned in surprise, dark hair swirling around her face. She had brown eyes, pink cheeks and a look of fascinated surprise as she looked him over.

"Hi!" she said breathlessly.

"Hi," he replied, reminding himself not to be taken in by a pretty face. She had been snooping.

"Are you…Killian?" she asked, looking hopeful.

"No."

Her face fell in disappointment.

"I'm Sawyer," he said a little defensively. "What can I do for you?"

The hope reignited in her eyes and was superimposed for a moment with sudden fear. Then she tossed her head as though she'd reached a decision and stuck out her hand.

"I'm China Grant," she said, wrapping her slender fingers around his with surprising strength. "I think…I mean…I believe I could be…your sister, Abigail."

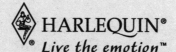

If you enjoyed what you just read,
then we've got an offer you can't resist!

Take 2 bestselling love stories FREE!

Plus get a FREE surprise gift!

eHARLEQUIN.com

For **FREE online reading,** visit
www.eHarlequin.com now and enjoy:

Online Reads
Read **Daily** and **Weekly** chapters from
our Internet-exclusive stories by your
favorite authors.

Red-Hot Reads
Turn up the heat with one of our more
sensual online stories!

Interactive Novels
Cast your vote to help decide how these
stories unfold…then stay tuned!

Quick Reads
For shorter romantic reads, try our
collection of Poems, Toasts, & More!

Online Read Library
Miss one of our online reads?
Come here to catch up!

Reading Groups
Discuss, share and rave with other
community members!

For great reading online,
visit www.eHarlequin.com today!

INTONL

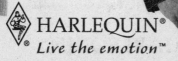

HARLEQUIN *Super* ROMANCE®

For a Baby
by C.J. Carmichael
(Superromance #1203)

On-sale May 2004

Heather Sweeney wants to have a baby. Unfortunately, she's in love with a married man, so that's never going to happen. Then one lonely night, she turns to T. J. Collins—who always seems to stand by her when her life is at its lowest point—and a few weeks later, discovers that she's about to get her greatest wish, but with the wrong man.

The New Baby by Brenda Mott
(Superromance #1211) On-sale June 2004

Amanda Kelly has made two vows to herself. She will never get involved with a man again. She will never get pregnant again. But when she finds out that Ian Bonner has lost a child, too, Amanda soon finds that the protective barrier around her heart is crumbling....

The Toy Box by K.N. Casper
(Superromance #1213) On-sale July 2004

After the death of an agent, helicopter pilot Gabe Engler is sent to Tombstone, Arizona, to investigate the customs station being run by his ex-wife, Jill Manning. Gabe hasn't seen Jill since they lost their six-week-old child and their marriage fell apart. Now Gabe's hoping for a second chance. He wants Jill back—and maybe a reason to finish building the toy box he'd put away seven years ago.

Available wherever Harlequin books are sold.

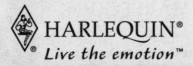

HARLEQUIN®
Live the emotion™

Visit us at www.eHarlequin.com

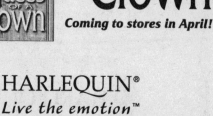

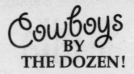
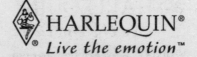